D1624080

DEADLY ANGEL

Kristi Holl

AnniesFiction.com

Library of Congress-in-Publication Data
Deadly Angel / by Kristi Holl
p. cm.
I. Title
                    2016933917

AnniesFiction.com
(800) 282-6643
Secrets of the Quilt™
Series Creator: Shari Lohner
Series Editors: Shari Lohner, Janice Tate, and Ken Tate
Cover Illustrator: Jonathan Bouw

10 11 12 13 14 | Printed in China | 9 8 7 6 5 4 3 2 1

1

Cabot Falls, Vermont
Present Day

Sofia Parker glanced up from the kitchen table where she waited for the icing on the petit fours to harden before adding frosting rosebuds. Her breath caught at the first glimpse of her twelve-year-old son, Luke, in uniform. A cloth-covered canteen and a leather pack hung from his shoulders.

Her hand went to her chest.

"What's wrong?" he asked, his brown eyes concerned.

"Nothing. You look very handsome, from the cap on your head to the shoes on your feet."

Luke pulled off the blue cap. "Forage cap, Mom, and they're brogans, not shoes."

"Right. Of course." The sleeves of the blue coat were a bit long, but the belt fit snugly, and it all looked genuine to Sofia. The heel plates on his square-toed leather brogans clicked on the tile.

"Won't your wool coat get hot today?" Sofia asked. They'd had record-breaking temperatures for Vermont this October, hitting nearly 80 degrees twice already.

"Wool's authentic," Luke explained. "Jason says that's the most important thing. The stuff inside this haversack looks real too." He dumped the contents onto the kitchen counter: a wooden comb, mess kit, New Testament, spiked candleholder, extra wool socks, and a folded sewing kit. "Jason bought these at other reenactments."

Sofia liked Jason, the friend who'd invited Luke to join his family at the St. Albans Civil War reenactment. St. Albans, site of the northernmost land action during the Civil War, was only thirty minutes from Cabot Falls. However, Sofia had been against Luke's participation at first. Twelve seemed too young to be involved in reenacting battles, even historically accurate ones fought with guns that shot blanks. But Luke had done his homework and showed her how many boys even younger than twelve had participated in the Civil War. They'd filled noncombat roles like drummers, fifers, couriers on horseback, runners, and water carriers. He'd finally won her over with how much he would learn about history.

Luke's eyes lit up at the food on the counter. "Man, you'll have a ton of leftovers today."

"I hope not," Sofia said, finishing the last row of diamond-shaped petit fours. "The lady organizing the tea said to expect up to seventy-five women."

When she and Luke had studied the events calendar a month ago, Sofia had noticed that there were also women's events scheduled at the reenactment. She hadn't realized that women participated, but the schedule included workshops on bonnet decoration, quilt patterns from the 1800s, music from the Civil War—and a ladies' tea.

Sofia had contacted the organizers about catering the tea, promising to research Civil War treats and make a variety of them. After agreeing on a fair price, she'd thrown herself into learning about garden party desserts during the Civil War period. This last week she'd baked and frozen cream-filled biscuits, lemon cakes, gingerbread, fruit-filled tarts, and petit fours.

She'd also researched Civil War reenactments and was astounded that there were so many in Vermont, let alone throughout the New England states. If she did well at St. Albans, she hoped the organizers would recommend her for other, larger events.

Footsteps thumped down the stairs, and ten-year-old Matthew skidded stocking-footed into the kitchen.

"Matthew, be careful!" Sofia cried as he slid near a box of cakes. They were ready to load into the pickup camper she was borrowing from her friend Marla.

Matthew sidestepped the boxes at the last moment. "Mom, why can't I react with Luke?"

Luke rolled his eyes. "It's *reenact*, not *react*," he said with exaggerated patience.

"Why can't I, Mom?"

"Matthew, we've been over this enough times," Sofia said. "You can watch the reenactment from the sidelines with all of us and go to some demonstrations with Dad. You'll hear a military band and see horses ridden by the cavalry." She pulled a tray of raspberry-filled tarts from the refrigerator to pack into containers.

"It's not fair," Matthew complained. "I'm the only one not getting dressed up."

"Dad isn't either."

"Yeah, but you and Vanessa and Wynter are. And Luke is. It's not fair."

Sofia laughed. "Your sisters would gladly trade places with you." It had taken much persuading to convince the girls to wear Civil War–style dresses and help serve at the tea. "Luke, run upstairs and tell your sisters to help me finish packing up the desserts. Julie and Marla will be here soon with the camper, and then we'll load up and hit the road."

Luke covered Matthew's curly brown hair with his forage cap. "Here, Matthew. You can wear this in the car." Then he scrutinized the cakes and grinned. "That little cake has a dent in it. Can I eat it?"

"Really? Drat." Sofia shrugged. "Sure, take it, but then you boys better get lost if you want to have a prayer of leaving on time."

Sofia, Vanessa, and Wynter were packing the tarts and sweetening the last jug of lemonade when a familiar voice rang out from the front hall. "Hellooo! Jim said to come on in," Julie Butler called, bouncing into the kitchen. Sofia grinned. With her infectious laugh and curly red hair, Julie never just came into a room. She made an entrance.

"Mouthwatering smells in here," added Marla Dixon, her other longtime friend and fellow Pinot Painter.

"Hi, girls," Julie said, hugging Vanessa and Wynter. "How can we help?"

"You could take my place and serve," seventeen-year-old Vanessa said promptly.

"And ruin her perfect nails?" Marla asked.

"No, really." Vanessa flung her blond hair over her shoulder. "I'd pay you. The last thing I want to do is appear in public in some costume with my hair in a bun."

"Oh, stop complaining," Wynter said, rolling her eyes. "It'll be fun."

"Yeah, *loads* of fun."

Sofia rolled her eyes. Vanessa and her fifteen-year-old sister rarely saw eye to eye. Sofia suspected they took opposite views on every topic just so they could argue. As the mother of one teenage boy, Marla had often remarked how much she enjoyed being around the girls. At times, Sofia would have been glad to loan them out for a day—or a week.

"This is fun, doing girly stuff," Marla said. "I love Tim, but camping and fishing get old after a while." Lean and athletic, she spent many weekends outdoors with her son. "I did clean out the truck camper. A bit of equipment is still in there, but I pushed it to the back."

"Oh, thank you," Sofia said. "The camper is a lifesaver. Renting a catering van would eat up my profits."

Marla handed over a set of keys. "It's not fancy. The windows are stuck shut. But there's plenty of room for your coolers." She wiggled the smaller key on the ring. "This one's for the little back door, but the lock's finicky. Tim misplaced the key on a trip last year, so he had to pry the door open. Now the door is a tad bent, and the lock sticks sometimes." She shrugged. "Frankly, I wouldn't even lock the back door, at least until you get the food out at the reenactment."

"Speaking of food, put me to work," Julie reminded her.

Sofia grinned. "You can pour the rest of the lemonade into those empty milk jugs. I'll serve it from glass pitchers the committee is providing, but I'm going to refill them in the kitchen from the jugs. The event organizers are providing dishes and will clean up afterward." Sofia pushed her light brown hair back off her damp forehead. If it was this warm already, she wondered what it would be like later in a long calico skirt, long-sleeved blouse, and shawl.

"I wish we could go today," Julie said. She and Marla both had prior commitments with their families. "But we'll be there tomorrow."

Sofia smiled. She looked forward to seeing the event through the eyes of an artist. At their last weekly meeting of the Pinot Painters, they'd made plans to take photos of the camp scenes, the quilters and other craftsmen, the military band, and the dressy ball in the evening. Then, throughout the winter, they could use the photos to paint pictures of various sizes. They'd sell them in the tourist art shops on the Cabot Falls square that took local art on consignment. If Sofia catered more teas around the state, she could probably sell some of the paintings there too.

Julie and Marla supported Sofia's efforts to build her catering business. She loved art for art's sake, but with four growing kids, her artistic endeavors—baking and painting—needed to bring in some money. Jim's high school teaching salary could only be stretched so far.

The Parkers, Julie, and Marla soon had the camper loaded. "Thanks, everyone," Sofia said, glancing at her watch. "I'd better go change." She gave Marla and Julie a quick hug. "See you tomorrow."

Sofia was grateful that her aunts, Rachel and Louisa, had graciously pooled their time and sewing talents to create period-accurate masterpieces for her and her daughters to wear. Sofia's blue print calico skirt, cream blouse, apron, lace shawl, and straw bonnet with pink ribbons were laid out on her bed. In five minutes she was changed, but arranging her hair under the crocheted hairnet proved more of a challenge. Finally she was ready. Glancing in the full-length mirror, she felt as if she'd stepped back in time.

She knocked on the girls' bedroom door as she passed. "Let's go, girls."

Jim and the boys led the way in the family Suburban while she and her daughters followed with the camper. On the way, her excitement built. She loved a new challenge. They arrived at St. Albans and found the park within an hour.

"Wow," Wynter said, leaning forward for a better look.

"Wow is right," Sofia agreed. A throng of people streamed toward the reenactment site. The spectators were easily distinguished in their jeans and tennis shoes, flocking into the park on this weekend of peak fall foliage. Sofia waited while several cavalrymen on horseback passed in front of them, harnesses jingling and saddles creaking. She had an odd sense of déjà vu.

Sofia drove the camper into the parking lot behind the Suburban. Everyone helped unload the food, bags of ice, and lemonade to carry across the road and up the steep hill. At the top was the historic brick building where the ladies' tea would begin at ten. The first battle sequence was scheduled for right after the tea. The reenactors were scheduled to perform several short battles on both days to show onlookers how Civil War battles were fought.

At the top of the hill, Luke grabbed Sofia's arm. "Mom, look!"

Sofia gazed out over the acres of wooded park below. Two groups of neatly arranged A-frame canvas tents looked like small towns. On the end closest to her, Confederate flags flew. At the far end, the Stars and Stripes—albeit a Civil War era one—waved over the Union camp.

Sofia closed her eyes briefly and absorbed the sounds of axes hitting logs, cavalry horses neighing, "generals" shouting orders, and a lone drummer boy practicing his cadences. For a moment, she was transported into the past.

"Isn't it neat, Mom?" Luke asked, eyes shining. "Can I go find Jason now?"

Matthew grabbed his brother's sleeve. "I'm going with Luke."

Sofia leaned down and looked into her younger son's face. "No, you are going to stay with Dad. Do you understand?" The crowd was huge already, and behind them across the road, cars were backed up, waiting to park. "Do you understand me?" she repeated.

"You already told me a hundred times." His tone bordered on surliness.

Jim came back outside of the brick building and ruffled Matthew's hair. "Don't worry. We'll stick together." He rolled up the sleeves of his plaid shirt and gave Sofia a quick kiss. "Good luck with the tea. We put the food and drinks in the kitchen."

"Thank you. See you later." She waved as Jim headed with the boys down the hill toward the battlefield.

Inside, Sofia was glad to find the tearoom already arranged. A dozen mismatched wooden tables were surrounded by wooden folding chairs; other chairs were lined up along the wall. On the long serving table near the kitchen door were stacks of small glass plates, a cut-glass punch bowl, and glass cups.

In the kitchen, Sofia and the girls unpacked the desserts and arranged them on trays covered with paper doilies. Then Sofia placed them on the tearoom's serving table, adding a pile of her business cards beside them. "The ladies will get their plates and a few mini desserts when they pass by the table. Once they're seated, you girls will circulate among the tables with extra desserts and pitchers of cold lemonade. Refill your pitchers from the milk jugs in the kitchen." She put more business cards in the front pocket of her lace-trimmed apron. "If anyone asks who made the food, I'll give them a card."

They were set up fifteen minutes early when three musicians, dressed in Yankee uniforms, entered the hall. They greeted the Parkers, then headed to the far corner where three chairs were grouped. Vanessa and Wynter watched them unpack two fiddles and a banjo. Back in the kitchen, Sofia listened as they played. Her heart stirred at *The Battle Hymn of the Republic* and *Dixie*, and she was almost misty-eyed at the poignant *Lorena*.

"Mom, come here," Wynter said, peeking in the kitchen. "There's a display at the other end of this building called 'The Stories Behind the Quilts.' They have quilt squares for sale too."

Sofia glanced at her watch. "I'm tempted, but there's no time right now," she said. "I'll definitely get there later."

Sofia knew firsthand about stories being stitched into quilts. She possessed one such quilt herself, which she had inherited from Nonna, her beloved Italian grandmother who had helped raise Sofia and her sisters after their mother's death. Each of the twelve different squares in the center of the quilt was of great historical significance. Sofia had been entrusted with the quilt and the quest of discovering where each square had come from.

A leather-bound diary written in Italian had accompanied the quilt, and Nonna claimed it contained enough clues to find the answers. Sofia had tracked down the origins of half of the silk squares so far. While Sofia's translation skills had grown, she'd only deciphered a few words and phrases regarding the next square: Positano, the name of a seaside Italian village; the names Marco de Luca and Febe; Fredericksburg; *Albergo Unione*, "Union Hotel"; and *amicizia*, "friendship." Sofia hadn't yet figured out who had stitched *Signed in wartime, 1862* at the bottom of the square. Marla, as head librarian in Cabot Falls, was doing some research for her. Once this catering job was finished, Sofia would have time to focus on it again.

At ten o'clock, no one had arrived for the tea. Sofia pushed down her anxiety as she double-checked the serving table. The music trio continued its Civil War melodies. She sent Wynter to the front door to watch for ladies headed their way. She was back in a few seconds.

"Mom, come quick."

Frowning, Sofia and Vanessa hurried to the front door. Out on the grass, twenty or thirty women in period day dresses, parasols up for shade, stood in groups of three or four.

"Why aren't they coming in?" Vanessa whispered.

"I don't know." Sofia wondered if she was supposed to make some kind of announcement.

"Look." Wynter pointed. "It's Abraham Lincoln."

Sure enough, climbing the rise was President Lincoln, wearing a long black coat and stovepipe hat. The gaunt, bearded man looked so much like photos of the real president that it took Sofia's breath away. Clinging to his arm was a Mary Todd Lincoln impersonator, short and plumpish, dressed in a lavender flowered gown and fingerless lace mitts, and carrying a parasol. Her hoopskirts swayed, and the fringe from her shawl fluttered, adding to her elegant appearance. The pearl comb in her hair and the painted fan dangling from her wrist set her apart from the other ladies.

Sofia and her daughters stepped back as the Lincolns approached the hall. The crowd of ladies waiting in front parted for them. Lincoln bowed to them all and then delivered his "wife" inside to a seat in the center of the tearoom.

At Lincoln's appearance, the fiddlers abruptly dropped *Lorena* and struck up *Hail to the Chief*. Lincoln nodded to Sofia, then walked out with quiet dignity. The other ladies and a few younger girls poured into the hall in a swirl of day dresses in every color. Sofia carried a plate of pastries to where Mrs. Lincoln sat at the most prominent table.

Others started down the serving line, where Wynter ladled lemonade from the punch bowl. Vanessa circulated around the room for refills from her cut-glass pitcher. The band continued with softer background music while the ladies' voices rose and fell.

Sofia smiled in satisfaction. The ladies were obviously enjoying her mini desserts, and they took more as the girls passed by with their trays. Hopefully some would pick up her business card.

From outside came the boom of a cannon and the popping of gunfire. Luke had said they'd be practicing before the battle. For a pretend battle, it certainly sounded real.

A touch on her elbow startled Sofia.

A wiry, grandmotherly woman leaned in conspiratorially. "She's crazy, you know," she whispered, nodding toward the center table.

"Excuse me?" Sofia asked.

"Mary Todd Lincoln. She's grief-stricken over the death of her son, and she suffers from migraines too."

"Oh. Yes. Of course." Sofia smiled as she realized the woman was speaking in character as a woman of the Civil War era. "I'm glad this is one of Mrs. Lincoln's good days."

Sofia took a doily-covered tray of desserts and wandered among the small tables. As she held out the tray for a group of ladies, footsteps pounded up behind her. She barely turned in time to prevent Matthew from colliding with her.

"Matthew! What are you doing here?"

"Dad said it's okay with him if it's okay with you," he panted.

Ladies nearby chuckled as Sofia cringed in embarrassment. Vanessa hurried over and grabbed Matthew's arm. "You're not supposed to be in here," she hissed.

"I had to ask Mom something!" he shouted over the music. When he yanked his arm loose from her grip, something flew from his hand.

"It's all right." Sofia picked up the carved wooden Union soldier, painted blue, and handed it back to her son. "Let's go into the kitchen, Matthew."

Matthew's eyes sparkled with excitement. "I got invited to be an extra."

"An extra what?" Sofia glanced out the door. "And where's Dad?"

"He stayed to watch Luke."

Sofia pushed down her annoyance. She'd been very specific about Matthew staying with one parent or the other at all times. Jim shouldn't have let Matthew take off alone through the crowd, even if it wasn't that far away.

"So can I, Mom? Can I?" Matthew hopped from one foot to the other.

"What exactly do you want to do?"

Matthew rolled his eyes. "Be an extra where there's a bank robbery by the Confederates. They did that here in St. Albans once, you know. I'm a kid with his dad at the bank."

Sofia remembered that the northernmost action of the Civil War had happened in St. Albans. About twenty Confederate soldiers had sneaked down from Canada to surprise the Yankees on October 19, 1864, robbing three banks in St. Albans for more than $200,000 in revenge for Union soldiers burning Southern cities. "You won't be shooting guns?" she asked.

"No, so can I?"

"I guess so." She mussed his hair affectionately. "Just be careful."

"Thanks, Mom." He ran off before she could ask Vanessa to walk with him.

Sofia hurried to the front door and watched Matthew run back down the hill. In the short time since the tea had begun, the crowd had thickened. Squinting, she kept her eyes glued to Matthew as he zigzagged through the spectators below. "Jim, where are you?" Sofia muttered, searching the crowd for her husband's blond hair.

She stepped aside as a few ladies left the building. The wiry grandmother chirped "Wonderful food" as she slipped around Sofia and started down the hill.

"Mom?" Wynter tugged at her arm. "Some girl spilled a whole glass of lemonade."

"I've got paper towels in the kitchen." When Sofia looked back at the crowd, she'd lost sight of Matthew. Uneasy, yet chiding herself for being overprotective, Sofia went to clean up.

Half an hour later, while Sofia and the girls were boxing up leftovers, Jim and Luke popped in. "Good," Jim said. "Looks like you'll get to see the first battle. It starts in fifteen minutes." He looked around. "Where's Matthew? What did you decide about him being an extra?"

Sofia froze, her hand in midair. "What do you mean, where's Matthew?"

"Isn't he here?" Luke asked. "When he didn't come back, we figured he stayed up here to mooch food."

Don't overreact, Sofia told herself firmly. She took a deep breath, but it felt like her heart had stopped. "I gave him permission, and he took off to find you. He was only here for five minutes." She clenched her fists. "I watched him from here till he got to the bottom of the hill."

Jim frowned. "He never got back to us."

Sofia couldn't comprehend what her husband was saying. She stared at him hard. Ten-year-old Matthew had apparently entered the milling crowd of strangers—and *disappeared*.

2

St. Albans, Vermont
December 1862

Phoebe Ashford arranged the remaining evergreen boughs over the fireplace, inhaling the scents of balsam fir and woodsmoke. Her touch lingered on the heavy wooden picture frame in the center of the mantel. How proud her husband had been the day he traded his wheelwright's leather apron for the Sharpshooter uniform of the Green Mountain Boys. George was fighting somewhere in Virginia, but Phoebe dreamed of him walking through the front door for Christmas.

She knew it was a pipe dream. Even so, she was determined to make this a memorable Christmas for their children.

Phoebe smiled over her shoulder at her son and daughter, who sang *Deck the Halls* along with Phoebe's best friend, Jane Stickle, while decorating the Christmas tree. John, already taking a man's role at eleven, had swelled with pride at cutting down the small tree by himself. While December 8 was a little too early to decorate the tree, it was good for them to focus on the spirit of Christmas.

Phoebe treasured John's kindness toward his sister, Annie, who just turned nine. She was a restless soul adjusting to a girl's restrictions. Annie was the child who longed to be with her father in Company F. She even talked of joining the new faction of women spies if the war lasted that long. Phoebe herself had no desire to wander from hearth and home. She'd be happy to never travel outside Vermont.

Jane pulled a wooden stool over to the tree, held her long skirts aside, and climbed up. "Phoebe, can you hand me the candles?"

"Of course." Candle stubs for the tree were an extravagance, but they wouldn't be lit until Christmas Eve.

"Mother, John's eating my share of the sugar cookies." Annie blocked his way to the red Christmas plate.

"There's more in the pantry, but go easy on them, or we'll have nothing for Christmas."

They raced past her, and Phoebe laughed as she raised the box of candles high.

Jane gazed after them wistfully. "Thank you for letting me join you this holiday season," she said. "Our house is too quiet." Her own husband was away fighting too, and they had no children. Jane had traveled by train from Shaftsbury in southern Vermont to St. Albans.

Phoebe gave her friend's hand a squeeze. "Consider this your home too. Having children around, while noisy at times, keeps my thoughts occupied and the worry about George at bay." His letters were few, and she battled far more fear than she let on.

Jane fixed the first candle to the end of a tree branch, straightening it until it was upright. "Sewing my quilts helps me," she said. "When I focus on them, I don't ruminate so much on how long it's been since we've had any news."

Phoebe understood. "I'm amazed how many quilts you've donated to the aid society," she said. "Think of all the fighting men right now who are kept warm by one of your quilts." The soldiers desperately needed not only warmth in the dead of winter, but something not infested with disease or lice.

"You're even busier, with your volunteer work and caring for the children too."

Phoebe studied her husband's picture on the mantel. "Volunteering comforts me when I can't directly help George."

As a member of the Ladies Hospital Aid Society, Phoebe helped prepare supplies that were delivered to battlefields and camps. Sometimes she nursed recuperating soldiers in private homes, but she couldn't take her children with her, so that was limited. In his infrequent letters, her husband called her "Fee-Bee," saying she was busy as a bee. She truly wanted to help the soldiers, but if she was honest with herself, the demanding days also meant that she fell into bed at night too exhausted to do more than pray before falling asleep.

Phoebe handed Jane another candle. "If you didn't stay with the children sometimes, I couldn't do half of what I do."

"You know it's a joy," Jane said, "since I wasn't blessed with my own."

Shrieking with laughter, Annie and John raced back into the parlor, telltale cookie crumbs around their mouths. Phoebe couldn't scold them though. Their joy did her heart good, and after all, it would be Christmas soon.

Jane had just started a round of *Jingle Bells* when a sharp knock on the front door interrupted them. "Keep singing," Phoebe called as she went to answer it.

On the snowy porch stood an older man, his shoulders hunched against the sharp wind. "Letter, ma'am," he said.

"Thank you."

Handing it over, he pulled his coat collar higher and tromped down the steps.

Back in the warm parlor, Phoebe grinned and waved the envelope.

Annie squealed. "From Father?"

Phoebe went to the fireplace and angled the envelope toward the light, then sighed in disappointment. "It's not your father's handwriting. I'm sorry." She slit open the envelope. Squinting, she read the lines quickly and sank into a chair. Hand shaking, she read them again in silence.

Mrs. Ashford, the note read, *your husband was critically wounded at Fredericksburg. Hospitals full in Virginia so transported to the Union Hotel Hospital in Wash., D.C. Come if you can. It never should have happened.—His friend, James Breckinridge.*

"Phoebe? You're white as a ghost."

Phoebe handed the note to Jane, then gathered her children close in a tight hug. "Your father's been wounded again, but this time it's serious." She swallowed hard. "He's in a makeshift hospital in Washington." She shivered suddenly. She knew from her volunteer work about the deplorable conditions in sheds, stores, and hotels turned into hospitals and how few nurses there were for the thousands of wounded. "I must go to him."

Jane gripped her shoulder. "I'll stay and care for the children. We will be fine."

Her own throat aching with unshed tears, Phoebe held her crying daughter tighter while John stood stiff at her side. "Thank you, dear friend." This was not the happy Christmas she'd envisioned for her children. Now neither parent would likely be here, and their father was wounded.

Jane reached into her voluminous sewing bag. "Please take George this quilt I finished yesterday."

"I will." Phoebe stroked the distinctive quilt top. Jane always made the center square from the remnants of tattered blue and green silk flags their Green Mountain Boys brought home. "Thank you."

Phoebe truly was grateful for her friend's gift, but she would have given anything if there were no need for it.

That night, with a heavy heart, Phoebe said goodbye to the children as she tucked them in tight. She would be down at the St. Albans train station before sunrise, ready to board the first train that had room for her. She gave them each one long last hug. Only the good Lord knew when they would be together again.

After allowing herself a good cry on Jane's shoulder, Phoebe straightened and dried her eyes. "Thank you from the bottom of my heart for staying with the children. I know they will be well with you."

Focusing on the task at hand, Phoebe packed her battered carpetbag. Sleep eluded her until close to morning, but she arose with one goal—to get safely to George in Washington, D.C. She'd never traveled alone, and secretly, it frightened her. But she'd done many hard things since the war started, things she'd never expected to do in her lifetime. She could do this too.

Dressed in her cavernous black bonnet and fuzzy brown coat, Phoebe tucked the package of gingerbread Jane handed her into her pocket. "For your travels," Jane said, hugging her.

Pulling away in the hired wagon, Phoebe was touched by the glint of tears in Jane's eyes, but her friend staunchly stood smiling and flapping her apron till Phoebe could see her no more.

The windy ride across town was frigid and jarring. The St. Albans railroad station, constructed along two tracks, was a combination passenger and freight depot built for the Vermont Central Railroad. Gripping her bag, Phoebe made her way with pounding heart to buy her ticket. In the early morning darkness, she bumped against big boxes and bundles of leather, was nearly annihilated by descending bales of cargo, and received growls from aggravated freight men. The shadowy station was a far cry from the cheerfully bustling place that she remembered by day.

Hunched men in dark coats with hats pulled low huddled in the doorways she passed.

"Lord, please protect me," she whispered, "and help me get a ticket soon."

The wait seemed interminable. Yet, after only two hours, Phoebe boarded a train heading south. She fought the panic that rose within her. The note from James Breckinridge had been written three days ago. Perhaps George was dead even now, and had died alone. But no, she wouldn't think like that. She would arrive in time to nurse him and, if allowed, to bring him home to Vermont to convalesce.

She fervently wished his friend had been able to send a telegram. She could have been in Washington already. Phoebe understood why the government had taken over the telegraph offices for military use. Even so, she hated that most families had to wait for long casualty lists to know the fate of loved ones. At least she'd heard within three days. Thank heavens the train from Washington had carried James Breckinridge's letter to her.

Finding a seat by a window and not too far from the car's water jar, Phoebe wrapped her shawl more tightly around herself, then buttoned her coat over the shawl. The lamps had been blown out when the sun rose, but she sat beneath one anyway. It would take two days to reach Washington, and she wanted to be near a light during the nights.

She clutched her soft carpetbag close. Later she would reread George's letters that she'd brought along. But for now, she was simply grateful to be on her way. The train was crowded, but she didn't mind. It was taking her to George.

As the train rolled down the rails and took curves at what felt like an alarming speed, Phoebe stared out through sooty windows. Having never been out of Vermont, she wondered if she'd be able to tell when the train crossed state lines.

The hours and the miles melted into each other. Even by the next day, the country through which Phoebe passed did not seem so very different from that which she had left. It was more level and less wintry, but sodden. Wayside encampments made the fields colorful with blue coats and the sparkle of buttons. Military laundry flapped and fluttered on the fences as the train rumbled by. Pots steamed in the open air. Several boys—*so young*, Phoebe thought—threw their caps into the air as the train passed.

Fear for her husband rose up in her at every turn, and Phoebe fought back by rereading his letters to hear his voice. Most of the letters were entertaining, since he'd known the children would be reading them too—stories of camp life and funny descriptions of the food. The last page of each letter was more serious, for Phoebe's eyes only, like his description of a recent day of battle.

> *Hundreds fell on every side, but I am still spared unharmed. I think I never knew hunger, thirst, and fatigue before—but I lay down that night under one of our faithful guns and blessed God that He had given success to our arms and spared your husband, your children's father. Take good care of yourself. Walk out often with John and Annie, and do not let anxiety on my account depress your spirits. I have sent you a flower that I plucked on the battlefield after a skirmish with the enemy. God bless you in all things, my darling wife and children.*

In the middle of the second day, Phoebe was jolted awake from a nap by a great commotion. She stared at the man across from her in alarm. "What's happening?"

"Train accident. An iron coupling broke," the slim, beak-nosed gentleman said. "The last car was detached accidentally from the train and left behind."

Along with the other travelers, Phoebe craned her neck to see out the window as the train slowed. "Do we have to go back and get it?"

"No, we just wait," he said. "It will catch up to us."

Two minutes later, it did, with a crash that knocked everyone forward. Several elderly ladies screeched. Men's hats flew off, Phoebe's bonnet was flattened, the overhead lamp fell into her lap, and the water jar turned a somersault, spraying her skirt as it rolled by.

Phoebe stayed in the car, but the men got out and stood about while the coupling was being fixed—getting in the way, from what Phoebe could see. She knew such accidents were common on the rails, but she yearned to be on their way. She was conscious of every minute that she wasn't getting closer to George.

Once the train was moving again, Phoebe began to prepare herself. Washington, D.C., wouldn't be anything like St. Albans; of that she was certain. And thanks to the delay while they were fixing the coupling, it would be dark by the time the train pulled into the station.

Phoebe's anxiety rose the closer she got to the nation's capital. When she finally arrived, the hustle and bustle of the train station left her dizzy and dismayed. Then a benevolent porter directed her to a stagecoach, and she gave the driver the name of her destination.

Though she'd been told that Washington was large and spread out, its magnitude took her breath away. The Capitol looked just like the pictures that hung in every boardinghouse and hotel next to the portrait of George Washington. She leaned forward when she saw the White House, all lit up, with carriages rolling in and out of the great gate. Pennsylvania Avenue, with its lights and music and military band, made Phoebe feel as if she'd landed in a carnival. All the gaiety seemed wrong somehow, with her husband lying wounded not far away.

She huddled back in her seat, longing for her children and the quiet fireside at home. Then she shook herself. She was where she needed to be, where she *wanted* to be. She prayed she wasn't already too late.

The stagecoach pulled to a stop in front of the hospital. It had been built as a hotel two years before, but now, during the war, it had been converted for the use of the Union army. Nothing Phoebe had seen while nursing in private homes prepared her for the assault on her senses when she walked through the front door of the Union Hotel Hospital. A mixture of the vilest odors that ever attacked the human nose took hers by storm. She wished she'd heeded Jane's advice to keep a handkerchief sprinkled with cologne on her person at all times.

"Excuse me," she said as an orderly rushed through the lobby. But her words were swallowed up by footsteps running up and down the wide stairway, the banging of pails, the cries of the wounded, and doctors calling for nurses.

Where is George? Phoebe ventured farther into the lobby and peered into the first room to her left. The former ballroom was now filled with cots placed side by side, with barely enough room to walk between them.

A nurse holding a tray of bandages, ointments, and towels came out of a room opposite, and Phoebe turned to her. "Excuse me, please. Please!" she called.

"Yes?"

"My husband, George Ashford, was brought here from Fredericksburg three days ago and—"

"Many were brought here that day, ma'am," she said gently. "I don't recognize your husband's name. Let me find the ward master for you." She pointed to a scarred wooden chair. "Please wait here."

"Thank you." Phoebe sank gratefully onto the chair, shivering in the drafty room. While it must have once been an elegant lobby, the carpet was now in shreds, the chandelier had only three unbroken glass lamps, and the open banister was missing several of its wooden balusters, leaving gaping holes where an unwary person could fall through.

The minutes crawled by. Phoebe stood and paced the width of the room. At every new footstep, she whipped around, only to find another nurse or orderly rushing by. She wouldn't wait much longer before she went looking for George on her own. He was somewhere in that building, and he didn't even know she had arrived. He could be slipping away from life—

"Mrs. Ashford?"

Phoebe whirled around so fast that she nearly fell. The uniformed soldier reached out and grasped her arm to steady her.

"Yes," she said. "I was notified that my husband, George, was brought here three days ago." She swallowed hard. "The note said I should come right away." She hesitated. "Is he . . . is he . . . ?" But she couldn't finish her question.

The soldier pointed her down the hall. "That room with the paper tacked to the door is for the more serious cases. Just go on in."

Phoebe ran down the hall, paused before the closed door to draw a deep and painful breath, then pushed it open. The large room was dim, with only a few candles burning. When her eyes adjusted, she realized that everyone was bedded down for the night. Fighting queasiness, she peered around the room of wounded soldiers. Slowly she started down the rows of beds, searching the faces of the men. She bumped into a cot.

"Ma'am?" a voice from the bed called.

Phoebe leaned closer, then quickly glanced away. The lump under his blanket clearly showed he had just one leg.

"Ma'am, who're you looking for?"

"My husband, George Ashford."

The soldier's lips pressed together; whether at her husband's name or the pain he was in, Phoebe couldn't tell. "Down there by the window is where they put him, but . . ."

Phoebe rushed off, peering through the dimness, but the bed at the end by the window was empty. Her heart nearly stopped.

Where is George?

"Excuse me," said a woman's voice behind her. "You can't be in here. Please come with me."

Phoebe whirled around. "They've moved my husband. Why? Is he in surgery?" Her voice rose, and her words sounded strangled. "Is he dead?" She swayed momentarily and sank onto the end of the cot. It was as she'd feared. He'd died alone, without her, before she could get to him.

"Please come with me. We'll talk in the hall. Let the men rest now."

Phoebe followed the nurse into the hall. "I'm sorry. I was told my husband, George Ashford, would be in that room."

"You've come a long way then," the nurse said sweetly. "I'm Nurse Alcott. Your husband was moved this evening to a . . . private room. Come this way."

"A private room? Why?" Phoebe followed the nurse down a narrow passageway to a closed door at the end. "Is he contagious with something?" Phoebe knew infections ran rampant through the camps and hospitals.

"He's in a tiny room. When this was a hotel, it probably held dishes and silverware in its built-in cupboards."

"Is he in quarantine?"

The nurse stopped and turned. She was homely, Phoebe thought, but she had the most compassionate eyes she'd ever seen. "No, he's not quarantined." She licked her lips. "Mrs. Ashford, I'm afraid that even though he is in and out of consciousness, he is under house arrest."

"Arrest?" Phoebe frowned. That made no sense.

"Yes, he has been accused of a serious crime. Desertion."

"No, he was wounded at Fredericksburg."

"Actually, according to a report we received today, he wasn't wounded there. It was north of the fighting somewhere. He may have been on his way home, what the military call 'absent without leave.' He was seen. He was shot twice while trying to escape—not wounded in battle."

Phoebe stared at the nurse, uncomprehending. "Shot by someone on our side, you mean?"

"Yes. One bullet hit the back of his left shoulder, one the back of his left thigh."

"That isn't possible," Phoebe said faintly. "There's been some horrible mistake. If he was north of the fighting, he was there for a good reason. He is a sharpshooter, after all."

"I only have the report given to me by an ambulance driver who saw it happen," the nurse said. "I'm sorry."

"That driver must have been mistaken." Phoebe shook her head as if to clear the confusion. "What is done with deserters?"

The nurse hesitated. "Officially, desertion is a capital offense punishable by death, but the number of deserters has been so high that President Lincoln said we couldn't execute dozens of our own men, especially when we're losing them by the hundreds in battle. But he will be punished. Many are branded with a *D* on the hip." The nurse gripped Phoebe's arm. "Execution is unusual now. The president grants amnesty to many soldiers who agree to return to their units."

Phoebe's head was spinning. *Branded a deserter? Amnesty?*

Then it hit her. Had she put so much pressure on George in her letters, longing for a united family at Christmas, that he'd gone absent without leave for his family? She shook her head in disbelief. She didn't believe one word of it. She knew her husband. George was innocent, no matter what any report claimed.

But how in the world could she prove it?

3

Cabot Falls, Vermont
Present Day

Matthew, missing? Where in the world could he be? Sofia refused to believe it. "He probably went straight to the site of the bank robbery scene. He was so looking forward to it."

"That's where I waited for him, Mom," Luke said, desperation creeping into his voice. "But he didn't show up. I thought he was with Dad, but Dad never saw him again either."

Sofia stared woodenly at Jim, knowing that both her fear and her anger probably showed in her eyes.

Just then, the speaker outside crackled, and a voice boomed over the park. "Attention. In ten minutes, we'll begin the first battle of the St. Albans reenactment. Spectators, find a seat on the sidelines. Actors, move into place."

Sofia ran outside and scanned the view below. It was such a short distance from the hall to the battlefield. How had Matthew disappeared so fast?

Sofia jogged back inside and down the hall to the tearoom. "Girls, please pack up any leftovers and take them to the camper. If you can get the backdoor key to work, lock up." She dug in her skirt pocket for the keys. "Vanessa, I'll get the keys from you later. When everything's cleaned up, just wait here for us."

The girls nodded, and Sofia hugged them both quickly, then turned to run outside.

"Sofia, wait," Jim said, grabbing her arm.

She took a deep breath, forcing herself not to jerk her arm free. Matthew was missing thanks to Jim. *Why couldn't he have done what I asked and stayed with Matthew?*

"What?" she asked.

"Try not to worry. I'm sure he's down there watching or with the bank robber group. We just missed him, I expect."

Sofia closed her eyes briefly and prayed for patience and calm. "I hope you're right."

On the way to the battlefield, they walked along the grassy corridor through the Confederate camp. A row of canvas A-frames with their tent flaps folded back lined both sides of the lane. Sofia glanced from side to side, peering inside tents where quilts covered narrow cots. Women in long skirts perched on canvas camp stools as they cooked with cast-iron skillets, and children poked at fires with sticks of kindling. As one woman reached for a metal coffeepot, the gray smoke shifted and swirled upward, stinging Sofia's eyes.

"We'll find him, Mom," Luke said. "Don't worry."

Sofia took a deep breath. She hoped fervently that she was overreacting, doing what Vanessa called her "mom thing."

She forced a smile for her older son, who'd so looked forward to this day. It wasn't his fault Matthew had wandered off. "What do the actors do when they aren't fighting?" she asked.

"Pretty much what real soldiers did," Luke said. "During the war, not that much time was spent fighting, but the work was hard and never ended. Soldiers had to police the camps, clear woods to build roads, dig trenches to fight in, care for their horses and mules, fix equipment, cut wood, and find water they could drink . . ."

Sofia only half listened as they moved through the camp. "He's not here," she finally said, trying to keep panic from her voice.

Jim pointed. "Let's try the battlefield next."

For the next fifteen frantic minutes, Sofia and Luke searched the crowds on one side of the battlefield while Jim headed to the spectators on the other side. They met at the south end of the field. Now Jim looked more serious. "He wasn't with the bank robbery group either," he said.

Sofia shaded her eyes against the sun. How big was this park anyway? Twenty acres? Fifty? Where else could he be? *Dear God, help us find Matthew.* Turning, she spotted something else and sprinted for it. "Come on!" she called over her shoulder.

A pair of uniformed St. Albans policemen in helmets and padded bicycle shorts were going by on mountain bikes. Sofia bet they got around fast in a crowd, a lot faster than in a car or on foot. And fast was what they needed right now.

Jim passed her and flagged down one of the police officers. The officer got off his bike and removed his helmet, revealing the most electrifying red hair Sofia had ever seen.

When Sofia and Luke caught up to them, the officer was reassuring Jim. ". . . so common to run off with a friend. Kids love to hang out where they keep the horses or at the sutlers' tents where they sell food and toys."

"Sergeant Poole, this is my wife," Jim said.

"Hello, ma'am. Does your son have a cell phone?"

Sofia shook her head. "No, but he's memorized both our numbers. He knows enough to borrow a phone and call us." She'd made sure Matthew could recite their numbers that morning. She'd wanted to safety-pin the information to him, but he'd protested. So far, though, the phone in her skirt pocket hadn't rung.

The officer flipped a notebook open. "Give me his name and description and your phone numbers, and we'll mobilize some backup to search immediately."

Jim gave a physical description.

Sofia dug in her calico skirt's deep side pocket. "And I've got a photo you can have." She reached for her billfold and pulled out Matthew's most recent school picture. She should have snapped a photo of him that morning on her phone, but she described his clothes for the officer. "We've already searched around the battlefield and in the camps. He hasn't been seen since shortly after ten."

The two officers conferred and quickly came to agreement. The second officer placed a call as Sergeant Poole turned back to them. "My partner is arranging an Amber Alert."

Sofia gasped. "You think he was kidnapped?"

"No, but it's our policy to thoroughly investigate all reports of missing children and get the word out immediately. The alert will be broadcast at least every thirty minutes for two hours, then once per hour or more after that."

"Good, thank you," Jim said, wrapping an arm around Sofia.

"Before the battle starts, we'll use their PA system and ask Matthew to return to the broadcast booth here." Sergeant Poole shook their hands. "Try not to worry. We return a lot of kids to their parents at these reenactments."

"There you are!" shouted a boy's voice.

Sofia whirled around. But it was only Luke's friend Jason, who ran up and grabbed her son's arm. "Come on. They're gonna start in a minute."

"I don't know . . ." Luke hesitated.

Sofia opened her mouth to say they needed his help to search. It had been over an hour since Matthew had headed down the hill to his dad.

Before she got the words out, Jim said, "You go on now and have fun. You know Matthew. He'll turn up."

Sofia's mouth snapped shut. While Sofia didn't want Luke's day to be ruined, she thought Jim should have asked him to stick around and help, especially if their children were going to make a habit of disappearing today. There were so many places in this huge park Matthew could be. *Unless he's been abducted and is already gone.* No, she couldn't think like that.

She bit her tongue. Jim wasn't showing nearly as much concern as she thought he should. Every instinct inside her said that Matthew hadn't just wandered off.

She shivered despite the heat. *Where is he?*

Washington, D.C.
December 1862

During her first two days at the hospital, Phoebe shivered at George's bedside in his closet-like room. One hour blended into the next. George was delirious with fever, and he didn't recognize her the two times he came around.

Phoebe didn't leave his side for more than a few moments at a time. She soon realized that as an alleged deserter, he received minimal care. While she couldn't claim that her husband was entirely forgotten, she had no doubt that his care was left to the very end. If Nurse Alcott hadn't brought some food on a tray and changed the dressings once, Phoebe wouldn't have known they were in a hospital. It would be up to her personal nursing to prevent George's leg from being amputated and to see that he didn't die from infection.

Making sure he lived came first. Clearing him of the desertion charges would have to come second.

On the third day, after sponging George's face and arms repeatedly to cool his fever, Phoebe groaned softly at the pain in her back. Shivering around the clock in a wooden chair was the hardest work she'd done in a long time. George seemed to be resting more comfortably. At least he had stopped thrashing so much. She took the opportunity to peek under the bandage on his leg and was horrified to see the red streaks that meant infection.

Too frequently, infection meant death.

Phoebe immediately went in search of a doctor to examine George's leg. Out in the lobby, orderlies hurried by, carrying a stretcher with a long white figure on it, his face shrouded. Phoebe felt for the hurting family who would be notified of that death, and she thanked God again for allowing her to care for George.

Spotting a doctor strutting through the lobby, she swallowed her fear and blocked his path. "Dr. Kauffmann?" she asked, glancing at his name badge.

"Yes, what?" he snapped. "I'm busy."

Phoebe avoided his piercing squinty eyes and concentrated on his failed attempt at a moustache. "My husband, George Ashford, requires a doctor. His leg's infected and—"

He pivoted and stomped away.

The second doctor she approached—a Dr. Bertram—was a short man with a fringe beard peppered with gray. His manner was more cordial, but he assured her that the nurses would notify him if special care was necessary. Then he hurried on.

Phoebe paused at the commotion coming from the ballroom, then peered inside. It held forty beds, and a dozen new wounded had just been delivered to fill the beds of those who had died. The new patients huddled around the great stove, ragged, gaunt, pale, muddy to the knees, and bundled up in ragged blankets and bandages that had obviously been worn many days. Nurses bustled around the new patients, calmly getting them settled and starting the washup.

No nurses would be available for George, not for many hours.

Sighing, Phoebe turned and bumped into a young man. His dark hair and skin, black eyes and eyebrows contrasted sharply with his white coat. "Pardon me," she said automatically.

"You need something, no?" His voice was thickly accented but understandable. "I can help you?"

"I wanted a doctor to check my husband, but they're busy."

The young man smiled in sympathy, revealing a perfect set of teeth. "*Si*. All surgeons are operating at the moment, but I will give *il messaggio*—er, a message, when one is free. You are Mrs. Ashford, no? A long way from home?"

Phoebe nodded, wondering how he knew. "Yes." She hesitated. Both his looks and his accent marked him as Italian. "You're a long way from home too."

"Yes, I come from small Italian village called Positano. I am Marco de Luca."

"I'm glad to know you, Dr. de Luca."

"Ah, no doctor yet. I am student and study *medicina* with Dr. Bertram. When war breaks out, Dr. Bertram invites me come here with him. He says I learn more in one month here than year in classroom." He spread his hands wide. "But they call me 'doctor' so soldiers not mind I treat them."

Phoebe could understand that. "And when the war is over?"

"I go home. My village is dying. I will be their *medico*."

"Good luck." Phoebe sincerely hoped the young medical student made it home. "Thank you for delivering my message. I'll wait in my husband's room."

Two hours later, when no one had come to examine George, Phoebe ventured out again, this time for food. So far she'd only coaxed George to take some broth when he was conscious. She stood aside for a stout washerwoman carrying an armful of clean but ragged uniforms and blankets. Avoiding Phoebe's eye, the woman stacked her load on a cart in the hall.

Phoebe wondered if she could take an extra blanket for herself. Jane's quilt helped George stay warm, but she herself felt like an icicle after a long night in a room with no fireplace.

"Excuse me, where do the blankets come from?"

The woman squinted angrily at Phoebe, arms crossed. "The uniforms and blankets are taken off dead soldiers. I make them ready for the poor wounded souls who come here in filthy, infested clothing."

"I see." From the woman's hostile expression, Phoebe knew she'd best not take a blanket. She would make do wearing her shawl and coat.

On her way to the kitchen, Phoebe glanced into the ballroom and was amazed at the transformation that had taken place. The ragged group of wounded from around the stove were now clean and tucked up in cots. Water, shears, and clean clothes had transformed even the roughest-looking ones from ragamuffins to heroes, albeit heroes with cropped heads.

Trays of bread, meat, soup, and coffee appeared from the kitchen. Nurses and attendants became waiters, serving abundant rations to all who could eat.

Nurse Alcott waved at Phoebe. "Did you get your husband some food yet?" she asked. "Broth? Bread to soak in it?"

"I'm on my way to look for some."

"Here." The nurse gave her a large bowl of soup and a thick slice of bread. "You eat whatever your husband can't manage."

Phoebe's eyes teared up at her generosity. Except for Nurse Alcott and the young Italian doctor, she hadn't had a truly kind word since she arrived. She had been branded a traitor too, it seemed. And she was no more a traitor than her husband was. "Thank you so much."

The nurse squeezed Phoebe's wrist, then moved on with her soup bowls and bread. Phoebe had just settled into her husband's room when there was a knock on the door. The young Italian stuck his head in. "You like *caffè* to make you warm?"

Phoebe was confused for a moment. *Oh. He means coffee.* "Yes, please. It's cold back here with no fire."

He handed her a cup, glanced at her husband's sleeping form, nodded, and backed out.

Phoebe held the metal cup, grateful for the warmth. But when she sipped the scalding liquid, she wanted to spit it out. The muddy liquid had a pervading flavor of molasses, scorch, and the tin pot it was made in. She decided to hold the cup and enjoy the warmth while it lasted, then pitch the coffee.

At one point, Phoebe drifted off, but she sat up with a start when the door banged open. The doctor who'd ignored her earlier stood in the doorway.

"I'm Dr. Kauffmann."

"I'm grateful that you're here, doctor," Phoebe said. "I don't like the looks of my husband's leg wound."

The doctor's jaw clenched in a rigid square. "Has he been conscious yet?"

"Not much. He doesn't speak. He's not sleeping as peacefully as he did yesterday either."

The doctor snorted. "Deserters have no right to sleep peacefully."

Phoebe gasped. She waited in silence while he examined her husband's wounds, feeling both intimidated and angered by his brusque manner.

His examination appeared perfunctory to Phoebe. "Should I be doing anything different now?" she asked as he straightened up.

"Keep the bandages wet so they don't stick to his wounds." He turned to leave. "I won't waste my time on a deserter. He'll only be executed later."

Phoebe glared at the doctor. "Please keep your erroneous opinions to yourself."

Dr. Kauffmann's eyebrows flew up in surprise. He left, closing the door harder than was necessary.

Phoebe sank back against the hard-backed wooden chair, closed her eyes, and tried to stop shaking. She opened her eyes finally to see her husband's gaze focused on her. He licked his parched lips. "Thank you." He closed his eyes, sinking back into unconsciousness. None of Phoebe's words of love and encouragement could awaken him.

He spoke once. It will happen again, Phoebe promised herself as she began his nighttime routine.

Her heart was lighter as she washed his feverish face, wetted the wounds, propped him on his good side, smoothed his quilt, and sang a lullaby that had been her children's favorite years ago. Perhaps he could hear her, even if he didn't respond. By eleven, the last labor of love was done. Phoebe found all the reward she could want in the peaceful look on her husband's face as he slept.

The following morning, George's fever felt higher, and Phoebe spent the morning cooling him with sponge baths. For now, the frigid room was a blessing. She waited desperately for him to speak to her again.

She wanted clean sheets to replace his sweat-soaked ones, but she was afraid to ask. Maybe she could volunteer to do his laundry herself. Apparently the washing woman had refused to launder George's filthy uniform, which still lay in a heap under his cot. *Well, I would be proud to,* Phoebe thought defiantly.

Two days later, George's fever finally broke. When Phoebe found his forehead and neck cool to the touch, she broke down and wept from relief and exhaustion. She knew the alarming statistics, how few soldiers pulled through infections. More died from infection than from the immediate effect of their wounds.

"Don't cry," came a hoarse whisper.

"Oh, George." Phoebe half cried and half laughed, feeling slightly delirious herself. "You're going to live."

"I have to tell you something," he said, his voice cracking.

"Let me get you some water first."

"No. I need you to understand . . . what happened." He plucked at the quilt, growing more agitated.

Hoping that talking would relieve his mind, Phoebe pulled her chair close. "I'm listening."

"You will be shocked." He closed his eyes briefly. "I wasn't shot in the fighting."

Phoebe gripped his hand. "I know. They told me."

George stared in disbelief. "You know?"

"Yes. The night I arrived, I was told you were shot while running away." She glanced around the tiny room. "You're under house arrest . . . for desertion."

George struggled to sit up, but fell back. "I wasn't deserting."

"I never believed them," Phoebe said, "but a report arrived that said so."

"I'll tell you what happened." He coughed once, then again, and Phoebe gave him a sip of water.

"Take your time," she said.

"I was in the fighting at Fredericksburg. I helped load wounded into ambulance wagons." He closed his eyes and drew several shallow breaths. "I saw an ambulance driver sneak several bottles of morphine into his pocket. Then he told a doctor tending the wounded that there wasn't any more morphine."

Phoebe frowned. "Why would he do such a thing?"

"It's an ugly side of war," her husband said, wheezing. "Some doctors and soldiers are morphine addicts, whether from pain, no sleep, or grief." He paused longer, breathing hard. "Stolen morphine gets sold to the highest bidder. It's morphine that our wounded are desperate for."

"That's horrible," Phoebe said. "But how did you get shot?"

He shuddered. "That ambulance driver saw that I'd witnessed the theft," he said bitterly. "So in all the noise and confusion, when I turned to lift the next wounded man into the ambulance wagon, he pulled out a pistol and shot me. He hit my leg first, then my shoulder, and then he dragged me behind a tree and left me to die."

"Why didn't anyone help you?" Phoebe cried, outraged.

"It was dark. There was yelling and chaos, and he probably expected me to bleed to death before anyone found me."

Phoebe gripped his hand. "It was an ambulance driver who reported that you were picked up north of the fighting, trying to make your way home. He said scouts found you and shot you when you wouldn't come back to your unit."

George's breathing was labored, and his eyes were filled with anxiety. "But you believe me, right?"

"Of course I believe you, George."

"Then you have to find the ambulance driver who shot me."

Phoebe blinked, then frowned. "How?"

"Sooner or later, he'll come here again, bringing more wounded. I don't know his name, but I can describe him for you." He coughed, and the wheezing sounded worse. "He had big arms, a broad, square-shaped face, and he is in his twenties, but he looks older because he's going bald." He closed his eyes as if to think harder. "His sleeves were rolled up. When he was dragging me out of sight, I saw his rattlesnake tattoo."

Phoebe shivered. *A rattlesnake tattoo?*

Her husband clutched her arm. "You must find this man, Phoebe."

Phoebe tried to sound confident for her injured husband, even though she had no idea what to do or where to start. "I'll find him. I promise."

4

St. Albans, Vermont
Present Day

"We'll find him, Sofia," Jim said after Luke left to line up for the battle. "We will."

When Matthew didn't show up at the broadcast booth, Jim continued his search near the battlefield while Sofia jogged behind the row of Confederate tents and back up the hill to the brick hall. At the top, she bent double to catch her breath, then hurried inside.

"Did you find Matthew?" Vanessa asked. "We heard the announcement on the loudspeaker."

Sofia shook her head. "But we talked to the police who patrol the reenactment, and they're searching already." She decided not to scare them by mentioning the Amber Alert. Wynter hugged her. "We took the leftovers to the camper. There wasn't much. The lemonade was gone."

Vanessa handed over the keys. "We'll help in the search now."

Sofia pressed her lips together. "You have your phone?" Vanessa nodded. "Okay, then you and Wynter can go together. No exceptions, understand?" The fun, friendly crowd felt menacing to Sofia now. "Call us if you find him. Or we'll call you if we do." She met her girls' eyes squarely. "Stick together."

Outside, Sofia phoned Jim, but he hadn't found Matthew yet or talked to anyone who'd seen him. She hung up, scolding herself for not getting the police officer's number.

First she headed toward the Union camp, wishing she'd kept Matthew's photo. The pictures on her phone were so tiny. Sofia worked her way down the row of Union tents, which looked just like the Confederate tents to her. A whiff of food—stew, maybe—reminded her that it would be lunchtime soon, but she couldn't imagine eating or even being hungry until she found her son.

At one tent, under an overhanging canvas porch, six or seven women in period costume were decorating straw bonnets. A folding table held a few dove feathers and some pink ribbon. At one woman's feet, a little girl in a calico dress was playing with a carved wooden puppet that danced on the end of a stick.

"Excuse me," Sofia said, "but have you noticed a small boy wandering around alone? He's about this high—" she held out her arm "—and he's wearing jeans and a green T-shirt."

The women shook their heads, one by one. "When did you see him last?" one asked.

"An hour ago, maybe a bit longer."

"If we see him, we'll tell the park police."

"Thank you." Sofia headed farther into the camp, vaguely aware of fiddle music and bursts of laughter. Though surrounded by hundreds of people, she felt incredibly alone.

Sofia jumped when a cannon exploded, followed by multiple rounds of gunfire erupting from the direction of the battlefield. Wisps of gunpowder smoke rose slowly in the azure sky, gathering into vapory clouds. Even though Luke had assured her that the actors used blanks in their Enfield and Springfield rifles, she could see why the deafening explosions made earplugs necessary.

After studying the map of the park on the back of the events list, she headed around the base of the hill to an open area where craftsmen were demonstrating nineteenth-century skills.

When she arrived, Sofia was surprised at how crowded the grassy area was. Not everyone came for the battles apparently.

She headed down the lane, searching for Matthew. Everything in her wanted to hurry, but Matthew was short; she couldn't risk overlooking him in the crowd. She forced herself to slow down.

At one spot under a shade tree, a plump woman was creating apple dolls; several peeled "heads" were hung up to dry. Next came a spinner making yarn on a spinning wheel, followed by a group of young girls braiding hemp rope. Matthew wasn't among those watching.

Under the next tree was an older woman, quilting on a rough-cut log frame while she answered questions from spectators. Sofia peered closer. Yes, it was the older woman from the tea who had told her Mary Todd Lincoln was suffering from grief and migraines. Unsurprisingly, Matthew wasn't part of her audience either.

Farther down the lane, Sofia's heart beat faster when she spotted a man who carved and painted wooden Civil War soldiers. Matthew had been carrying a Union soldier just like the one he was carving. Hope soaring, she eagerly showed him Matthew's photo on her phone. "He must have bought a toy from you. Do you remember him?"

The man squinted at the tiny picture. "I don't recognize him. My toys are for sale in the sutler tents too. He could have bought it there."

Sofia swallowed her impatience. "Where else might little boys go?"

He talked around the pipe clenched in his teeth. "The cavalry keep their horses over there." He motioned over his shoulder toward a grassy, roped-off area. "They give the young lads rides sometimes. Always boys hanging around the horses." He whittled facial features into the tiny soldier in his hand. "Of course, the cavalry's in the battle right now, but check the horses later if you still haven't found him."

"Thank you. I will."

As she moved on, a frantic pressure built inside Sofia. She dialed Vanessa first. The girls hadn't seen Matthew. She called Jim then and could barely hear him over the sounds of cannons and rifles. No, he hadn't spotted Matthew, and no, the police hadn't called him. Sofia told him about the carver's advice to check the horses after the battle.

"Good idea," Jim agreed before hanging up.

Fighting hopelessness, Sofia continued down the lane to where vendors sold caramel apples, caramel corn, and funnel cakes. Sofia would have given anything to share a funnel cake with her little boy right then. Her heart ached as she listened to a family laughing in the shade of a brilliant red maple.

If she didn't find her youngest child unharmed soon, life might never be that carefree again.

Washington, D.C.
December 1862

Will I ever feel safe again? Phoebe was consumed by that fearful question all during the long, cold night as she replayed George's story of being shot in the back. He thrashed and moaned in his sleep as if telling his story had taken what little strength he'd mustered.

By morning, she knew one thing: Finding the ambulance driver alone wouldn't help. He'd simply deny everything George claimed and call it a wild invention designed to save him from execution.

By midmorning, George was awake again. While he claimed to feel better, every movement caused him to tighten his mouth, and beads of moisture appeared on his forehead.

"Phoebe, listen." He reached out his hand. "I've been thinking. A friend of mine was wounded at Fredericksburg. I talked to him just before I was shot. It's very possible that he witnessed it."

Phoebe held her breath. *At last.* "Who is it? He's probably somewhere in this hospital right now." There were at least six wards of wounded.

"James Breckinridge, and he was—"

"James Breckinridge. That's who told me to come." She dug to the bottom of her carpetbag for the letter. "He must have seen your attack. See? That's what he meant when he said it should never have happened."

George smiled for the first time since Phoebe's arrival. He fell back on his cot, breathing heavily. "James will vouch for me. He knows I wasn't running away. Ask a doctor where he is."

"Don't worry." Phoebe jumped up. "I'll find him."

With a lighter heart, she hurried down the hall to the lobby, but it was empty. She peered into the ballroom, but only nurses were in attendance. She had to find a surgeon or the ward master, someone with a complete list of the wounded. She checked each ground-floor room, the kitchen, the alcove by the medicine cupboard, and even the back garden, but she found no doctors. Were they all performing surgery? She ran up the broad staircase to the surgical floor, bracing herself for what she might see. Several closed doors on the second floor stopped her. *Now what?* She couldn't simply walk unannounced into an operating theater.

Before she could decide, one door opened. A surgeon emerged, his white coat splattered with blood. His large round eyes gave him a look of constant surprise.

"I'm Dr. Dickerson. Are you lost, my dear?" His smile revealed a mouthful of oversize incisors and canines.

"I need some information. Do you have a wounded man here by the name of James Breckinridge?"

"Why?"

"He witnessed who shot my husband. He can testify that George wasn't running away at all."

Attendants emerged from the other rooms, and he pulled her out of their way. "You must be Mrs. Ashford. According to our information, your husband was found north of the fighting and was shot as a deserter while escaping."

"That's not true!" Phoebe took a deep breath and willed herself to speak calmly. "The ambulance driver who wrote the report is the one who shot my husband. And there was a witness who—"

Dr. Dickerson cut her off. "Many brave men here will die from their wounds, no matter what we do. How do you think they feel about comrades who left them to the enemy? Traitors get no sympathy from any of us." He pivoted on his heel and returned to his surgery.

"My husband's not a traitor!" she shouted after him. More softly, she added, "He would never desert anyone."

She started back down the stairs to the lobby. Phoebe was outside George's room when she heard her name being called. She turned to find the young Italian medical student coming toward her. He, too, showed signs of having been in an operating room.

"Mrs. Ashford, wait, *per favore.*" He caught up with her. "I hear you talking to Dr. Dickerson. You want to find James Breckinridge, no?" He glanced over his shoulder. "I search master list. Breckinridge not here."

"He's not?" Phoebe couldn't keep the melancholy from her voice.

"Many Fredericksburg wounded *vanno*—go to other hospitals in the city. There are fifty-six hospitals here." He handed her a torn slip of paper. "Two such places we send overflow wounded."

Phoebe glanced at the names and addresses, then looked up. "Thank you." She hesitated. "Why are you helping me?" Clearly no one else believed her husband was innocent.

He waved a hand. "Things not as they appear sometimes."

"What do you mean?"

"I go upstairs before I am missed."

Phoebe watched him stride back down the hall and disappear.

Within the hour, with her bonnet tied tight and bundled up against the wind, Phoebe stood shivering outside the hospital. A horse-drawn cab would use some of her small money store, but it couldn't be helped. She couldn't walk the distance.

She handed the hack driver the address of the Armory Square Hospital, the closest hospital on her slip of paper, then lifted her skirts and climbed up. If James Breckinridge wasn't at the Armory, she could walk to the second hospital only six blocks from it.

Upon arrival at the Armory, Phoebe could see at once why Nurse Alcott spoke with such envy of those who worked there. The long, clean, warm, and airy wards were a wonder compared to the hotel's cold, often dirty, and inconvenient arrangements.

How she hoped George's friend was here. What a good place to heal. Phoebe was eager to thank James Breckinridge for writing to her, as well as to ask if he'd witnessed George's shooting. Even today she might verify George's story and remove the awful stigma from his reputation.

Phoebe stopped at a desk near the back. A small, bright-eyed, white-aproned lady was reading near a stove. A table full of trays and glasses stood off to one side, and a large, well-stocked medicine chest stood on the other. The Armory had order, method, common sense, and liberality, as opposed to the hotel's disorder, discomfort, bad management, and no visible head.

Phoebe inquired about James Breckinridge. The nurse

double-checked current and past records, then shook her head sadly. "I'm sorry, there's no soldier here by that name, and never has been."

Phoebe's breath went out of her with a whoosh. Her dejection was enormous. She forced a smile. "Thank you for checking. I have one other place to look." She showed the woman the next address.

"Ah, yes." The nurse gave Phoebe specific directions to the mansion-turned-hospital and suggested the safest route for a lone female venturing into the city.

"Good luck, dear. Are you his wife?"

Startled, Phoebe shook her head. "He's a friend of my husband's. They were wounded at Fredericksburg."

"As so many were."

Outside, Phoebe headed north. With the buildings closer together, the wind diminished. Phoebe could have enjoyed the mild December day—it was the 17th already—if she'd been on a sightseeing excursion. Instead, she picked her way around mud and had to step aside repeatedly for groups of soldiers being marched down the street.

Good heavens, she thought, *half the male population seems to be escorting the other half to the guardhouse.*

At last she turned onto a residential street. Two blocks later, she arrived at the address of the hospital. She navigated the long broken sidewalk and climbed the wooden steps to the wide veranda. Instead of the wicker furniture that Phoebe imagined had been there before the war, wheelchairs made of oak and caning were parked haphazardly. Right inside the etched-glass door, its glass still miraculously without cracks, she stopped a red-faced steward.

"Breckinridge, you say?" He flipped through pages clipped to a board. "Yes, he's in the nursery."

"What?"

He laughed, his grin splitting his round, flat face. "We have to designate the different areas, and James Breckinridge is in the former children's nursery. Of course, I'm afraid the room bears no resemblance to a baby's room today."

"Is it upstairs?"

"Yes. I'll find a nurse to take you."

As Phoebe waited by the front door, it was hard to stand still. She'd never expected that finding George's friend would be this simple. Surely he was mending. She doubted he'd be allowed visitors if he weren't.

A nurse appeared from the back of the house, wiping her mouth. "I'm sorry—you caught me eating," she said.

"I'm sorry."

"Quite all right." Her pointed chin and dark hair with its widow's peak gave her a heart-shaped face. She grinned as she stuck a biscuit in her pocket. "It wouldn't be there when I returned."

"The steward said you could show me to the nursery?"

"Of course. You're Mr. Breckinridge's first visitor."

"Will he be all right?"

"I'm no doctor," the nurse said, "but from the hundreds I've nursed, I'd give him a better than fifty-fifty chance. And a visit from a friend always raises their spirits." They started upstairs. "Don't stay long though. It can also tire them."

"I won't."

"Here you go," the nurse said a few moments later. "The nursery ward." She reached to push open the door.

"Nurse." A thin, harassed doctor with a bald head dotted with freckles snapped at her like a rifle shot. "Who's this?"

"A visitor for James Breckinridge."

"Who gave clearance for this?"

She hesitated. "I don't know. I just thought—"

"You're not here to think." He turned to Phoebe. "James Breckinridge isn't well enough to have visitors. You'll have to come back in a few days."

"I won't stay long, I promise."

"Did you hear what I said?"

Phoebe bit her tongue, swallowing her anger at his rudeness. She couldn't afford to make an enemy here. "Yes, I heard, and I'll come back in a few days."

Without acknowledging her reply, he pushed into the nursery ward and firmly closed the door behind him.

"I'm sorry," the nurse said, escorting Phoebe back downstairs. "Most of the doctors are respectful, but . . ."

"But some have rather an elevated estimation of themselves."

The nurse laughed. "Yes. Rather."

Weary and frustrated, Phoebe flagged down a hack cab two blocks away and settled into the hard seat to be bounced over potholes on her return. She hated to report to George that she'd found his friend but they wouldn't let her talk to him.

"Have you seen the statue?" the hack driver called over his shoulder.

"What?" Phoebe turned both ways to peer around her huge bonnet. "What statue?"

Her gaze followed where he pointed. It was the Statue of Freedom she'd heard about—a bronze statue of a female figure wearing a helmet decorated with an eagle's head and feathers. She held a sheathed sword in her right hand and a laurel wreath and a shield in her left. The statue had no pedestal as yet, but stood flat in the mud. Young boys made mud pies in its shadow. But high above the squabbling little throng, the sun shone full on Freedom's broad forehead, and some bird had built its nest in her wreath.

Phoebe leaned back as they passed on down the street. *Freedom. What a wonderful word.* Phoebe realized that she had always taken her freedom for granted. *Never again.* Now she wondered if her husband would ever again be free.

5

St. Albans, Vermont
Present Day

Sofia broke free from the crowd around the food vendors, and with the sounds of cannons and gunfire echoing behind her, trotted toward the sutler tents. The sides of a dozen huge canvas tents were rolled up to display the large assortment of goods for sale. During the actual war, Luke had told her, these tent stores sold things the soldiers really needed—leather goods, guns, camping gear, or articles for a soldier's haversack. *Now it's as commercialized as Christmas*, Sofia thought.

She ducked in and out of tents where fingerless mitts, sunbonnets, and hoopskirts were sold. Other sutlers sold candy, cheap plastic toys probably made in Taiwan, and overpriced "authentic" tin cups and plates. Always, everywhere, Sofia scanned the crowds inside the tents and strolling down the grassy lane in between.

After checking the last tent—this one selling gray bratwurst that turned her stomach—Sofia leaned against a tree trunk for some shade.

Matthew, where are you?

Glancing down, she spotted a wadded-up calendar of events on the ground and smoothed it out. The wrinkled schedule listed events for the rest of the day, right up to the late-night military ball.

Then a notice at the bottom of the schedule jumped out at her: *Real doctors and nurses will staff a medical tent at the reenactment.*

Minor first aid will be administered there. The fire department's social hall half a mile south will be available for patients, and two ambulances and plenty of emergency medical service personnel will be on-site.

Sofia had noticed parked ambulances earlier in the day. Had they transported anyone to the hospital? She had a sudden vision of Matthew walking behind a cavalry horse, getting kicked in the head, and being taken, unconscious, to a hospital. Or maybe he got too close to the gunpowder when a reenactor loaded a cannon. He tended to ignore safety rules when it interfered with his fun.

"I've got to find that first-aid tent," she whispered.

Walking back down the lane toward the crafters, Sofia dialed first her husband, then Vanessa. The girls were searching in the camps, talking to kids Matthew's age, but so far, no luck. Jim hadn't spotted him yet either, despite circling the battlefield three times and talking to spectators, but Sofia was glad to hear more concern in his voice. He didn't sound quite as certain that Matthew had just wandered off.

Near the quilting lady, Sofia spotted Sergeant Poole, thanks to his bright red hair that stood out like a beacon. His bike leaned against a tree, and he was talking to a small group of kids about staying safe and "stranger danger."

Sofia stood at the edge of the group in the shade, shifting impatiently from one foot to the other. Why wasn't he out looking for her son instead of standing around, chatting? Shouldn't he be putting up flyers with Matthew's picture on them or something? Even as she thought it, she knew it was unfair of her. The police were doing all they could. Kids often escaped from parental supervision, and they were usually found unharmed.

But this wasn't just any child. This was *her* child.

As she waited for Sergeant Poole to finish, she was vaguely

aware of the quilter talking to the spectators around her frame. "This blue quilt is made from the uniforms of one woman's husband and son. The silk squares were made of remnants of their blue-and-green battle flags of our own Green Mountain Boys. Many women worked out their grief by quilting," she explained.

Sofia glanced her way and then did a double take. The square she pointed to was nearly identical to the quilt square Sofia had at home that Marla had been helping her research.

"Hello."

Sofia jumped and whipped around to find Sergeant Poole at her elbow. "Did you find Matthew?" he asked.

"No." Sofia gritted her teeth, trying to keep her emotions in check. "Are officers still searching?"

"Yes, in and around the park," the officer said, "including places where children could be trapped, asleep, or hiding."

Sofia took a deep breath at the word *trapped*. "Could you check the St. Albans City Hospital too? You know, in case he got hurt and was taken there by ambulance."

"I've already put in a call. Let me check." He pulled out his cell phone. Five minutes later, he shook his head. "No one by the name of Matthew or Matt Parker has been admitted to the local hospital or is in their emergency room. No unknown boys that fit his description have come in either. He wasn't seen at the first-aid tent. So that's good news."

"I suppose so," Sofia agreed.

She turned in a slow circle to scan the area. The only truly good news would be a call from Jim or Vanessa to say they'd found him.

Washington, D.C.
December 1862

Phoebe settled back in the hack cab and tried to shake off her displeasure at not actually meeting James Breckinridge. If that irritable doctor hadn't seen her, she might have been able to save George. She was oblivious to her surroundings until the cab slowed, then stopped in the street.

Oh please, she thought, *not more prisoners on the way to the guardhouse.*

A large crowd had gathered on both sides of the street, stopping traffic. "What's going on?" she asked the driver.

"Not sure," he said. He hopped down off his seat, talked to a man and woman, then climbed back up. "It's Mrs. Lincoln."

Phoebe sat forward eagerly. She'd love to catch a glimpse of the first lady. "Where is she?"

"In that house where the carriage is parked. I'll turn around and get you to the hospital."

"Oh, let's wait a bit." Phoebe couldn't help being enthusiastic. From her own volunteer work, she knew that the president's wife was devoted to the Union forces, despite her many relatives who supported the Confederacy. Phoebe had read in the papers that the war overshadowed all of Mary Lincoln's activities. She volunteered as a nurse in the Union hospitals and even toured Union army camps and reviewed troops with her husband. Mary Lincoln's Sanitary Commission fairs had raised private donations for soldier supplies like blankets; the Contraband Relief Association also raised private donations for the housing, employment, clothing, and medical care of recently freed slaves.

Just then, excitement rippled through the crowd, and the women on the sidewalks stood on tiptoe. Phoebe stared too.

Was the woman dressed in black coming out of the house really Mrs. Lincoln?

The short, stout woman nodded at the ladies around her and then held out her hand to be helped into her carriage. As she stepped up, she met Phoebe's gaze, nodded again, and then disappeared inside her carriage.

Phoebe sat back, stunned. The wife of the president of the United States had noticed her.

The crowd broke up after the Lincoln carriage departed, and Phoebe thanked the driver for waiting. "I had no idea I'd ever see Mrs. Lincoln. I understand that she entertains the troops encamped at the White House to raise their morale."

"There's them that say it's nothing to be proud of," the driver said, spitting over the side of the conveyance. "Criticism runs high against her. She gives extravagant parties during a time when many can barely feed their families."

Shocked, Phoebe leaped to the defense of her personal heroine. "Surely keeping up the morale of our soldiers is worth the expense."

He shook his head. "Not all her spending is on the troops," he said, bitterness creeping into his voice. "The condition of the White House didn't suit her when she moved in, and she spent $27,000—more than President Lincoln's salary—to fix it to her liking. What excuse is there for such lavish spending when soldiers don't have enough blankets?"

Or enough painkillers, Phoebe thought reluctantly. Disappointed at having her heroine tarnished, Phoebe settled back for the remainder of the drive to the Union Hotel Hospital. Phoebe had read Lincoln's famous speech about "a house divided against itself cannot stand." If his wife's spending was out of control, what about his own house? Would it stand?

It was only a week before Christmas, but Phoebe could see no signs of the upcoming holiday as she entered the hospital lobby.

She dreamed of sitting with George, warm at a fire, drinking coffee and eating Christmas cookies, watching the children unwrap their gifts—

"Look out, Mrs. Ashford."

Phoebe's head snapped up. "I'm sorry." She had nearly run into Nurse Alcott who carried a wooden box holding bandages, a basin of steaming water, and washing cloths.

"Was it a successful trip?" the nurse asked.

"Yes and no," Phoebe admitted. "I'd like to tell you about it. Do you get a break soon?"

"Not for a couple of hours. After you see your husband, come back. We can talk while I do the nightly tucking in." She shifted the box higher. "If you like, that is. I can see how tired you are."

"You're kind to notice, considering that I'm nursing one and you're nursing at least fifty."

"But I have a bed to sleep in," Nurse Alcott pointed out. "Now that your husband can be left alone for a while, I'll see about finding you a place."

Phoebe didn't know about sleeping away from George, but she looked forward to talking to the nurse. "I'll be back soon."

As she fed George some bread soaked in broth, Phoebe told him how her efforts had gone that day. George was cheered by the fact that she'd found his friend.

"I know James will vouch for me," he said again. "But I've been thinking, Phoebe. This is bigger than clearing my name. That driver is stealing morphine from doctors who need it in their surgeries, from patients who can't sleep because of the pain and so cannot relax enough to heal. He must be caught." He stopped, gasping for breath. "He's the traitor, not me."

Phoebe agreed and then described seeing Mrs. Lincoln. "She looked kind, and she volunteers with common people like me. This might sound far-fetched, but maybe I can enlist her help somehow to find out who's behind the morphine thefts. It can't be just one driver. He must be selling the morphine to someone."

George moaned as he shifted on his cot. "I wouldn't mind some painkiller myself," he said ruefully. "I don't know if Mrs. Lincoln would help or not, but people say she has more power in this city than anyone except the president himself."

It wasn't long before he drifted off again. Talking seemed to tire him so quickly. She had to remember that and not burden him with her other worries, like how long her money would last with having to hire cabs and buy her own food. She added her coat over his quilt for extra warmth, then stretched and rubbed her sore back.

Yes, a bed would be nice. Many more nights in that straight-backed chair and she'd require medical treatment herself. Then she shook her head, ashamed of the thought. How could she compare an aching back with the wounds and missing limbs of these soldiers?

It was dim in the ballroom later, with only a few candles burning. Phoebe started across the room to where Nurse Alcott was working. Then a voice stopped her. "Miss? Could I trouble you?"

Phoebe winced as she faced the young soldier. It looked as if he'd received a gunshot wound in the cheek. "What can I do for you?" she asked.

"Could you loan me a looking glass?"

She hesitated. "Um, let me see." Hunting in the supplies, she found a mirror with the shaving gear and handed it to the soldier.

He regarded his swollen face with a doleful expression. "That's too bad. I wasn't a bad-lookin' chap before, but now I'm done for. Won't that be a thunderin' scar?"

Phoebe's heart went out to him. "Rest assured, your sweetheart will admire any honorable scar as lasting proof that you faced the enemy." She smiled. "All women think a wound is the best decoration a brave soldier can wear." She continued down the narrow aisle between beds, hoping her own husband understood that.

Nurse Alcott had finished with one soldier and was moving to the next with warm water and clean bandages. She glanced up and grinned. "Glad you could join us for the party."

The men close by chuckled, and it was a welcome sound. As the nurse worked, Phoebe told her about finding James Breckinridge that day, plus seeing Mrs. Lincoln and what the hack driver had said. "It's not true, is it?" Phoebe asked anxiously.

"I'm afraid so," the nurse said. "I admire her war efforts. She works hard. But the overspending is also true. In fact," she said, lowering her voice, "things are worse than that. I've heard from someone reliable that—"

"Nurse, Tommy here's sick."

Nurse Alcott ran to the young soldier's bedside with a pan and held it until he finished. "There there, it's all right. Just a reaction to the medicine most likely."

Next was a soldier who needed a new dressing on his arm. "Another sad case," the nurse whispered to Phoebe as they approached him. "One leg gone, and the right arm so shattered that it may well follow. You'd never know it by his spirits though."

Taking a deep breath, Phoebe followed Nurse Alcott to the last bed in the row. The little sergeant greeted them in such a merry way that Phoebe would have thought his wounds hardly worth worrying about.

Phoebe kept her eyes averted, focused on his face, and chatted away while the nurse changed his bandage. The boy gave her a brave smile, though his lip quivered. "I never was in one of these places before, and I think this cleaning up is a jolly thing for us, though it probably isn't for you ladies."

"Not at all," Nurse Alcott said briskly. "The war can't be all fun and dancing with handsome soldiers. If there's a little cleaning up as well, we're happy to do it."

The idea seemed to tickle him, for he laughed cheerfully.

So did Phoebe, awed by his courage.

Half an hour later, Nurse Alcott finished "tucking in" her last soldier for the night. Her smile never left her face until she was out in the lobby and had closed the door to the ballroom. Then she sighed and collapsed on the bottom step of the staircase.

Phoebe sat beside her. "Can I get you some coffee?" she asked. The nurse shook her head. "What were you saying about Mrs. Lincoln when we were interrupted?"

"It's very sad, but not uncommon anymore." Nurse Alcott rubbed the back of her neck. "It's rumored that Mary Lincoln is using drugs to keep going since the death of her son Willie this past February."

"He was only eleven, wasn't he?"

The nurse nodded. "She uses a variety of drugs for her nerves and to help her sleep. She also suffers from migraines."

"That's awful." Even without migraines, Phoebe could imagine crying for relief if she lost a child of her own. Could it be that Mrs. Lincoln was one of those surviving on morphine? George had mentioned that some were addicted because of pain or lack of sleep, but also because of grief. The president's wife would only have to ask for it, and she could certainly pay if necessary.

"You've gone quiet." The nurse glanced sideways at Phoebe. Phoebe shook her head. "It's nothing."

She couldn't say it aloud. If the ambulance driver had stolen the morphine to sell to the highest bidder, who could pay more than the president's wife? If this scheme went as high as the White House, no wonder Phoebe's husband had been shot to keep it a secret. And if it were true, the one woman who might have the power to help her could also be determined to cover it up.

When Nurse Alcott headed up to her third-floor room for some rest, Phoebe was no longer sleepy. She paced up and down the hallway outside George's door.

The stakes were high for the ambulance driver. Having her husband witness the theft had been a small obstacle taken care of with two bullets. Since he'd survived to report it, making sure George was executed as a deserter would be next on his list. He couldn't do that alone, though. He'd need help, but from whom?

Phoebe shook her head in fear and frustration. She could no longer tell the heroes from the villains.

6

St. Albans, Vermont,
Present Day

Sergeant Poole had barely put away his phone before his radio squawked with an unrelated call and he pedaled off. Sofia started down the lane, but a cheery voice called to her.

"Hello, there. Your tea this morning was lovely," the quilter told her. "Best food I've had at a reenactment."

"Thank you." Sofia nodded toward her quilting frame. "Beautiful work." She pulled up a photo of Matthew on her phone. "I was wondering—"

"This is my copy of the Dear Jane quilt, the famous quilt made by Vermont's own Jane Stickle during the Civil War. It consists of 225 blocks, each in a different pattern. Jane stitched some words and dated it on the back."

Stifling her urge to snap at the chatty woman, Sofia held up her phone.

"You want a picture?" The older woman smiled.

"No, I want to show—"

"By the way, I'm Amanda Witte."

"I'm Sofia—"

"Parker." Amanda wiped her oval glasses on her skirt. "I picked up one of your cards." She tilted her head to one side and squinted. "Are you unwell, dear? If you don't mind my saying, you don't appear to be enjoying yourself today."

"You're right." Sofia showed her a picture of Matthew on her phone. "I can't find my younger son."

"The little boy who ran into the tearoom?"

Sofia's throat tightened. "That's the last time I saw him."

"He reminded me of my grandson." Amanda patted Sofia's hand where it rested on the quilting frame. "I'll keep a special eye out for him."

Just then the woodcarver called from across the lane, "Amanda, I'm going for lunch at the food tents. Can I get you anything?"

"No, I brought a cooler in my van."

"Say," the man said, noticing Sofia. "Aren't you the woman looking for her little boy?"

Sofia nodded. "I haven't found him yet."

He joined them at the quilting frame. "I heard that during the battle, a couple boys were taken to surgery."

"What?" Sofia cried. An emptiness cold as ice chilled her.

"Whoa there," he said. "I meant the medical tents run by reenactor surgeons. They 'operate' on the wounded taken off the battlefield. Spectators love their demonstrations."

"Thank you. Matthew's a real ham. He'd love to be part of that." Hope rose within her. "Which way to the surgical tents?"

The carver pointed, and Sofia took off at a run. She knew how badly Matthew had wanted to join Luke in the battle. He'd sulked when she'd said he was too young. It would be just like him to join the battle without permission. If Jim had searched for him on the battlefield itself, he wouldn't have seen him carried off on a stretcher.

Soldiers from the battle plus the spectators who'd been watching now streamed toward the sutler tents. Sofia plunged through the crowd, apologizing as she elbowed several people.

Around a curve, four large hospital tents appeared. Inside were bunks arranged dormitory-style. Outside, bandaged soldiers—complete with fake bloodstains, crutches, and slings—hobbled along the row of tents. Sofia stopped at the first surgical tent, pushed through the spectators, and stepped inside. The sight that met her eyes made her stomach roll.

Sticking out of a tin bucket by the operating table was a man's lower leg. A surgeon with a small saw stood by the operating table. His once-white apron was soaked with crimson blood.

Lightheaded, Sofia blinked several times before the truth registered. These were actors, and that lower leg drizzled with red paint was simply a plastic prop.

Sofia glanced around inside the tent, then backed out. Matthew wasn't on any of the stretchers or operating tables. When she stepped inside the next hospital tent, a fierce argument immediately broke out. The crowd closed in around her, blocking her view of some of the tables.

"Woman," an older surgeon thundered at a sturdy nurse, "remove yourself from my hospital! You have no business being here."

"No business?" She shook a finger in his face. "I've followed the troops and nursed them for more than a year."

The surgeon snorted. "Madam, the heat has affected your mind." He wiped his hands on his coat. "Where are your orders, woman? Show me papers assigning you to my hospital."

"I ignore Federal orders."

"Then by what authority do you work here?"

With painstaking precision, the nurse rolled up her voluminous sleeves, then pinned her skirt up out of the dirt. "I receive my authority from the Lord God Almighty. Have you any higher authority?"

Sputtering, the surgeon clamped his lips together, making his handlebar mustache quiver. The nurse moved in beside him to assist with the amputation.

The spectators applauded the skit and moved away, giving Sofia room to see. Matthew wasn't among the "wounded" in there either.

She ducked out of the tent. Weary resignation weighed her down as she searched the remaining stifling tents, where doctors shouted orders to nurses over the dramatic moaning of the wounded.

"Oh, Matthew, where are you?" Sofia whispered. Walking blindly, she caught her foot in the rope tied to a tent stake, tripped, and fell on the matted grass.

"Can I help you?"

Sofia shaded her eyes as she stared up into a scruffy face full of wrinkles. The hair around the fringes of the soldier's cap was white. "I wish you *could* help," she said, taking his hand. "My young son's disappeared." She showed him Matthew's picture and explained where she'd already searched. "I heard that two boys were carried off the battlefield and brought here."

"Yes, but they were older than your son—fourteen or fifteen." The soldier stroked his moth-eaten beard. "This is odd. One of our surgeons disappeared during the battle too. He left for the battlefield to bring back the wounded, but he never returned." The soldier wiped his glistening face with a bandana and tipped his hat. "I hope you find your son, ma'am."

Fighting back tears, Sofia called her daughters, then Jim. No news. "Let's all meet back at the hall on the hill," she told them. "We need a new plan. And we need it now."

Washington, D.C.
December 1862

Shortly after falling asleep, Phoebe's nightmare was interrupted by real moaning. It took her a dazed moment to realize it was her husband. She stood too fast, was dizzy for a second, and then reached his bedside in two steps.

"George, it's me, Phoebe. Darling, wake up."

When she brushed back his hair, she was alarmed to see how damp it was. The fever was back.

He thrashed back and forth, then lay still. Just when she hoped he had drifted back to sleep, his moans and thrashing returned.

No, not again. His fever had broken two days ago, and Nurse Alcott believed he'd beaten the infection in his shoulder. What could have gone wrong? Was his leg infected now? Or was it something else? She'd heard the nurses talking about typhoid fever. The symptoms included fever, chills, and weakness.

Phoebe fought back tears and tried to think calmly. *Poor George.* Branded a deserter, he'd only been offered a painkiller once. If he had some now, he might calm down enough to rest. As she stood by his bed, she had never felt so powerless.

With a pan of cool water from the kitchen, Phoebe spent the next two hours bathing her husband's head, neck, and arms. The room felt bitterly cold, yet she couldn't cool his skin. As soon as a doctor appeared downstairs in the morning, she would corner him and demand something for George's pain.

But the sun rose, the patients stirred, breakfast was served, and no doctors materialized. Phoebe watched orderlies trudge up and down the stairs with patients on stretchers. The surgical floor above must be teeming with the wounded, she suspected. Nurses flew by and washerwomen plodded past, but no doctors appeared.

Phoebe was in the hall when an attendant stopped at the medicine cupboard and unlocked it. After searching inside, he grabbed a white jar and then hurried back upstairs.

She pressed back against the wall and held her breath. Unless her eyes had deceived her, the attendant had forgotten to relock the cupboard.

Inching forward, she watched for nurses and orderlies. No one paid her any mind, and for once, she was glad to be invisible. She had seen Nurse Alcott give morphine pills to the wounded. Phoebe felt sure she could manage it herself.

She'd only take enough to help George rest. The pain kept him so agitated. A little painkiller, like the other soldiers received, would help him so much.

Phoebe sidled up next to the medicine cupboard, turned her back to the lobby, and opened the right-hand door. Inside was a small notebook. She glanced at it long enough to see that it listed the painkillers and numbers of bottles on hand. Reaching behind the notebook, she grasped a dark brown bottle that appeared to hold morphine pills.

Without warning, a hand grabbed her wrist while another wrenched the bottle from her grasp.

Phoebe cried out, then clapped a hand over her mouth. *Dear Lord, help me!* Then she whirled around and stared into the blazing eyes of Nurse Alcott.

"What are you doing?" the nurse hissed.

"I'm sorry," Phoebe whispered, feeling her eyes fill with tears. "Truly I am. I only wanted one pill for George." She swallowed hard. "His fever is up again, and he isn't given any painkillers like the other soldiers."

The silence stretched for what felt like an eternity. Phoebe knew that Nurse Alcott was required by conscience—and probably by law—to report the attempted theft. Would Phoebe be banned from the hospital and kept away from her husband now?

After an interminable time, Nurse Alcott shook out one pill, dropped it into her apron pocket, and returned the bottle to the cupboard. "Come with me."

In George's room, which only received dim light from a flickering, smoking stub of a candle, the nurse felt his forehead.

Then she roused him from his tossing and moaning. "Water?" she asked Phoebe.

In grateful silence, Phoebe handed her a tin cup still half full. The nurse tilted George's head up, placed the pill on the back of his tongue, and forced him to sip the water. He coughed a bit, but when she was satisfied that the pill had been swallowed, she laid his head back on his pillow.

She watched him closely. "That should help."

"Thank you." *And please don't report me*, Phoebe begged silently. She couldn't ask the nurse to cover for her, and yet . . . if they threw Phoebe out of the hospital, she couldn't protect George. Whoever had shot him twice wouldn't hesitate to try to kill him again, given the chance.

After a few minutes, George quieted and fell into a deep sleep. "I understand your feelings. It's hard to watch a loved one suffer. Morphine is being called the new wonder drug," Nurse Alcott said softly. "Doctors use it to relieve pain as well as to treat diarrhea and dysentery, the other big killers. And, like here, it sedates patients so they can rest enough to heal."

"It is a wonder drug," Phoebe agreed.

"But not without side effects." Nurse Alcott's voice sharpened. "Sometimes it's only nausea, but sometimes it can interfere with breathing." Her piercing eyes bored into Phoebe's. "I'll try to watch out for your husband more, but it is easy to overdose, so *never* try to administer morphine yourself again."

"I won't. I promise."

"Too much morphine use can lead to a habit, one the patient feels driven to satisfy. It's known as 'soldier's disease.'"

Phoebe understood. If wounded men or distraught women were driven to satisfy a need for morphine, whether for themselves or a loved one, it explained why the ambulance driver could command a high price for it.

Nurse Alcott studied Phoebe closely, as if trying to judge whether she could be trusted. Finally her frown cleared, as if she'd made a decision. "I've noticed morphine disappearing from the medicine cupboard from time to time. It could be a careless mistake—people in a hurry not marking it in the book. On the other hand, after what your husband says he saw—"

"That got him shot."

"Yes. It's made me think, but I can't put my finger on anything." She started for the door, then glanced at the wooden chair in the corner. "You've been sleeping there all week?"

Phoebe nodded. "Or sometimes on the floor by his cot."

Kindness returned to the nurse's face. "Your husband will sleep for hours now. You must rest, or you'll be sick too. Come to my room on the third floor. I'll bring you some tea and toast while you get warm by the fire. There's a spare cot right now in my room."

"You're so good," Phoebe said. "But aren't the rooms up there reserved for the staff?"

"Yes, but if Kauffmann reprimands me, I'll point out that you're nursing your husband, which saves us running down the hall to help him."

Phoebe didn't believe anyone was concerned about nursing George, but the offer of a bed in a warm room—even for a few hours—sounded like heaven. And she'd be a better guard for George if she stayed healthy and alert.

"Come with me," Nurse Alcott said. "I'll settle you in, but then I must get to work." She grinned suddenly, making her rather homely face pretty. "As long as we're to share a room, a first-name basis might be in order, Mrs. Ashford."

Phoebe smiled back. "I'm Phoebe from St. Albans, Vermont."

The nurse gave her hand a hearty shake. "I'm Louisa May Alcott from Concord, Massachusetts."

Phoebe followed Louisa up to the second floor, across a wide landing, and then up to the third floor. "This must have been servants' quarters in peaceful times," Phoebe said.

Louisa laughed softly. "It's still servants' quarters. We just wear different uniforms." She opened the third door on the left. "Welcome to my humble abode. You'll find it . . . well ventilated."

"I see what you mean." Phoebe stared in shock at the window. Five small panes of glass had suffered compound fractures; two were covered with rags. She could see a church steeple across the way through the other panes. She was thankful for the fire that blazed away at one end of the room, burning a huge log inch by inch, as it was too long to go in all at once.

"Make yourself at home. It's not fancy, but it's cozy."

Phoebe came in gratefully. The bare floor was scuffed and covered with dents and scratches. Two narrow iron beds with thin mattresses and thinner pillows were flanked by two rickety tables and two wobbly chairs. A mirror hung over a tin basin with a blue pitcher. A quick peek into the open closet revealed a varied collection of bonnets, bottles, bags, boots, and boxes.

Louisa nodded at the closet. "I leave it open. We have rats, and I always open it with fear and trembling after it's been closed up."

Phoebe cringed. *Rats?*

She hurried to stand in front of the fire. *Oh, the heavenly warmth.* She closed her eyes briefly and let it soak into her. As it thawed her stiff limbs, she slowly relaxed. She could almost sleep standing up. In front of her on the mantel, she studied clues about her new roommate: a flatiron, a Bible, a candle, a lavender bottle, a new tin pan, and two very fat black bugs, which seemed to have invited themselves.

A sharp knock sounded on the door. "Nurse Alcott?" called an orderly.

"Coming," Louisa answered through the closed door. "I'll be there as soon as I talk to Dr. Bertram."

Phoebe stifled a gasp. Despite being so friendly, would Louisa report her attempted theft after all? She was afraid to ask.

Louisa must have known what she was thinking. "I do have to report that the medicine cupboard was left unlocked, hopefully by accident and not by design. I won't mention you." She paused, then said pointedly, "I trust there's no need."

"No, I won't try that again," Phoebe assured her.

"Then no one else has to know."

After Louisa left for her shift, Phoebe pulled up a chair by the wonderful fireplace. She soon grew drowsy, then crawled onto her hard cot, where sleep mercifully pulled her into its bosom.

7

St. Albans, Vermont
Present Day

Fear threatened to overtake Sofia as she darted through the crowd around the reenactors' surgical tents. Scanning her surroundings more out of habit than expectation of spotting her son, she climbed the hill to the old brick hall. Her family already waited there.

The girls were finishing foil-wrapped sandwiches. Sofia realized that it was past lunchtime, and nearly three hours since Matthew disappeared.

"Here, Mom," Wynter said. "We bought you a pulled pork sandwich."

"No thanks, honey." Sofia was grateful, but a secret part of her wondered how any of them could be hungry or stop searching long enough to stand in line for food. Was Matthew hungry now?

Vanessa wiped her mouth. "We went through all those tent stores—"

"Sutler tents," Luke interrupted.

"*Tent stores,*" Vanessa repeated with a glare in his direction, "and all the eating tents and asked all the kids we could, but nobody remembers him."

"I checked the crafters—one man was whittling toys like the one Matthew had with him this morning—but no one there had seen him." Sofia kept her voice even and matter-of-fact with great effort. She didn't want to frighten the kids. "Just now I was at the surgical tents where they were doing skits. He wasn't there either."

Jim put an arm around her shoulders. "You're shaking," he said. "Here. Try to eat." He handed her a bottle of water and an energy bar. "We checked the horse enclosure after the battle, but he wasn't there, and he hadn't asked for a ride."

"Just now, when we came back through the camps," Luke said slowly, "I spotted this guy, and I remembered something."

"What?" Sofia demanded.

Luke shuffled his feet. "Before Matthew went to your tea to ask about joining the bank robbery, Dad let him go with Jason and me to the Union camp. There was a soldier . . ."

"Yes?" Sofia prompted.

"He was teasing him and trying to scare him."

"Bullying him, you mean?" Sofia asked. "Doing what, exactly?"

"Grabbing his wooden soldier and holding it out of his reach," Luke said, "and he tripped him and laughed when he fell. Matthew kicked him and got his toy back, but the soldier threatened him."

"What!" Sofia exclaimed. "Threatened him how?"

"That if he saw him in camp again he'd . . ."

"He'd *what*?"

"He did this." Luke made a jabbing motion. "He was holding his rifle with a bayonet attached."

A squeak of fear escaped Sofia's throat. A bayonet sounded more dangerous than a rifle! "Why didn't you tell us about him before?"

"Jason said he fooled around like that all the time. His friends were laughing too. But when I saw him in camp again, I remembered."

"Does Jason know his name?" Sofia asked.

Luke shook his head. "No, he's just seen him around at other reenactments."

Sofia gripped Jim's arm. "We have to find Sergeant Poole immediately." Oh, *why* hadn't she asked for his phone number?

"Now let's stay calm," Jim said. "You can't really think that some actor has hurt Matthew."

"I don't know what I think," Sofia snapped. "Maybe he's got Matthew tied up somewhere, bound and gagged in his tent as a joke or something."

Jim gazed at her with genuine sympathy, but for some reason, it annoyed Sofia.

"I'm not being hysterical," she said through gritted teeth, "but we have to report that soldier to the police."

"I agree," Jim said. "We'll find Sergeant Poole or another officer right away."

Without another word, Sofia turned and ran down the hill. Frustrated tears blurred her vision. If only Jim had kept Matthew with him like he was supposed to . . . if only she'd sent Vanessa with her son . . . this never would have happened!

Washington, D.C.
December 1862

One night's sleep in Louisa's warm room gave Phoebe a new lease on life. The next day George slept more deeply, and by the following morning, his temperature had dropped again. Louisa brought Dr. Bertram to see George, but the doctor didn't know if George was battling infection, fighting off typhoid, or something else. Whatever it was, Phoebe was grateful that he slept peacefully as she set off again to talk to James Breckinridge.

The hack cab kept up a brisk pace in the early morning frosty air. Phoebe was nervous, yet excited. If she could see James Breckinridge this time, the false accusation against George could be straightened out before the day was over. And if she cleared George's name, she saw no reason why she couldn't take him home to recuperate. *We might have Christmas together after all.*

Twenty minutes later, Phoebe was again on the veranda of the mansion hospital. She nodded to two older soldiers wrapped in blankets and bundled into wheelchairs. Inside, she found the steward and requested admittance to the nursery ward.

"Who'd you come to see?"

"James Breckinridge. I was told to come back in a few days."

The steward scratched his head, then shook it sadly. "I'm sorry, ma'am, but Breckinridge died yesterday."

"No!" She gripped the man's arm, and he guided her to a chair just inside the door. "The nurse said he was mending." Phoebe trusted nurses' opinions as much as doctors', since they had the closest contact with the wounded. "Check again, please. There must be some mistake."

"I'm sorry, ma'am. Disease and infection hit the wounded hard."

"Is that what happened?"

"I don't rightly know," the steward said, his voice gentle. "But I know his body was removed yesterday."

Phoebe gripped her gloved hands together and stood. "Thank you." When she turned to leave, Phoebe glanced up and spotted the nurse with the heart-shaped face coming down the stairs. Maybe she could give Phoebe more details. Phoebe raised a hand and waved, but the nurse spun around and hurried back up the stairs.

Crushed, Phoebe pushed open the door with the beautifully etched glass and stepped out onto the veranda. Hadn't the nurse recognized her? Or was she trying to avoid Phoebe?

She started down the wide steps, wondering how long it would take to find a cab.

"Ma'am?"

Phoebe turned to find an orderly tucking a blanket around a gaunt, hollow-eyed soldier. "Yes?"

He motioned for her to come closer. "I overheard you in there. Go to the dead shed if you want answers."

Phoebe recoiled. "What?"

"It's a shed that's been turned into a mortuary." He quickly gave her directions. "It's where Breckinridge was supposedly sent."

"Supposedly?"

The orderly raised his eyebrows significantly, then silently turned back to his work.

What would be the point of going there? Phoebe wondered. If George's friend was dead, he couldn't tell her anything. On the other hand, why didn't the staff here want to answer her questions? Were they covering something up about James Breckinridge?

Phoebe shivered. She'd come to see her husband's friend and she'd failed, unless she wanted to see him in a pine box. But she sensed that someone was hiding something. Breckinridge's unexpected death was too convenient for whoever was determined to get George out of the way.

She straightened her shoulders and found a hack cab to take her to the "dead shed."

Phoebe climbed into the cab with only one thought in mind. Had her husband's friend, the witness to his shooting, really died? She couldn't go back to George without knowing the truth.

The cab passed the stores and churches, moving toward the Potomac River where the warehouses lined up along the wharves, one after another. The wind shifted, and she nearly gagged. She covered her nose with a handkerchief. The slime from the river had smelled bad enough, but this was something else entirely.

"Is there a farm nearby?" she called to the driver.

"Naw. You're smelling the cavalry depot. Must have thirty thousand horses parked there, ready to supply the Army of the Potomac."

Phoebe tried not to breathe.

The hack slowed then and finally stopped. Phoebe paid part of what she owed and climbed down. "Please wait here for me. I'll need a ride back to a hospital." A shudder ran through her body, and she clutched the side of the cab for a moment.

Then she faced the long, low building, devoid of markings, with two doors on one end. There was something incredibly sad about having to put the Union dead in a warehouse. She was grateful for those working inside that it was the coldest time of year.

She knocked on the first door, waited, and then knocked harder. No response. She had the same luck at the second door. If she pounded any harder, she'd bruise her hands through her mitts.

Casting around on the ground, Phoebe found a broken brick and several chunks of wood. She grasped a piece of wood and beat on both doors. In less than a minute, the first door was flung open.

"What?" a heavily bearded soldier yelled. When he spotted Phoebe, he glanced both ways and then back at her, undisguised surprise and curiosity in his bloodshot eyes.

"I'm Mrs. George Ashford. I've come on my husband's behalf, looking for a friend of his. I was directed by an orderly to come here." She omitted the fact that she was actually there to discover if the man was truly dead. "I am—well, I'm here to identify him." This gruff man wouldn't know that she'd never set eyes on James Breckinridge.

Phoebe's knees began to shake. She hadn't actually considered the next part, but what if he let her come in? Could she face a warehouse of bodies?

The soldier riffled through a stack of papers and then shook his head. "Nope, no unidentified corpses here. He must have come already tagged. Looks like you came here for nothing." He moved to close the door.

"Wait." Phoebe had to find out if James was actually there. "Could you check your records and see if his family has been notified yet? I know it takes many days for casualty lists to be posted at the telegraph offices. My husband is in the Union Hotel Hospital, and he would like to write to his friend's family. Could you tell me the address listed for James Breckinridge?"

The man rolled his eyes but growled, "Wait here." He went in and slammed the door.

Phoebe waited outside, huddled near the building to stay out of the damp, freezing wind blowing from the river. She ached for the families of the fallen soldiers inside the warehouse, thankful that George wasn't among them. Wagons rumbled by in the lane; she hoped that none would stop with bodies while she was there. She was about to hit the door again when it was thrown open.

The bushy-bearded man held a bound book. "I've gone through the records for the last three days, just to be sure. There's no James Breckinridge on the list of received." He cleared his throat. "You must have misunderstood the message."

Phoebe stared in silence. She hadn't misunderstood the orderly, nor his directions. "Is this the only warehouse holding bodies?" she asked, glancing down the muddy street.

"The only one."

"I'm sorry to have troubled you," she finally said, turning back to the waiting hack.

What was going on? Had James Breckinridge been spirited away from the hospital when it became known that she wanted to question him? She'd been directed to the dead shed, but was it just a wild goose chase?

Or was the orderly trying to tell her that, somewhere in the city, James Breckinridge was alive?

8

St. Albans, Vermont
Present Day

Sofia had to keep searching. She sensed that somewhere in camp, her son was being held, perhaps by the actor who'd threatened him. As the Parkers neared the bottom of the hill, Sofia caught a movement down the lane. She ran ahead of her family, waving her arms wildly.

"Stop. Stop!" She reached the road as the uniformed officer hit his brakes. It wasn't Sergeant Poole, but it didn't matter. "My son is still missing," she gasped at him, out of breath from her run. "Matthew Parker? Ten years old?"

"Yes, Sergeant Poole gave us his description. We've been scouring the park, and the Amber Alert went out. Try not to worry. I'm sure he'll turn up. We've returned three missing kids to parents today already. There's so much to see, and they take off."

Sofia clenched her fists. She bet the children who "took off" were toddlers or preschoolers. "I just found out that our son was bullied by one of the soldiers in the camps, and the soldier actually threatened him." She gave a rapid account of what Luke had told them.

Her family had caught up with her, and now the officer glanced at Luke's uniform. "Was Matthew a drummer boy or something?"

"No," Sofia said. "He wanted to be in the battle, but I thought he was too young."

"Perhaps," the officer said slowly, "he was angry with you about that."

Sofia felt her blood pressure skyrocket. "He did not run away because he was mad. He's not hiding to get away from his parents."

Jim laid a hand on Sofia's arm, and there was a warning in his pressure. He must have known how close she was to giving this officer a piece of her mind. Other children might do such things to their parents, but Matthew would never worry them sick on purpose.

"You know your child best," the officer said, "but in this case, I hope that you're wrong and he comes back on his own."

Sofia nodded curtly. Admittedly, that would be the best-case scenario. She watched the officer ride away.

"Now what?" Luke asked, his voice sounding young, scared, and guilty.

Sofia felt her anger evaporate. She wrapped her arms around her son, scratchy wool coat and all. "This is not your fault," she said.

"We wouldn't even be here except for me."

She squeezed harder. "It's not your fault *at all* that Matthew is missing."

"If it's anyone's fault, it's mine," Jim said. "I shouldn't have let him out of my sight."

Sofia sensed her children silently wishing that she would say it wasn't their father's fault either, but she couldn't choke out the words. "I should have made him stay at the tea until you came for him, or sent one of the girls with him back to you," she finally said.

Vanessa wiped her sunglasses on the tail of her shirt. "What do we do now?"

Sofia tried to sound optimistic as she let go of Luke. "Keep looking, keep asking questions."

Luke straightened his coat. "Dad and I will go back to the Yankee camp and try to find that soldier."

Jim's face was grim. "We'll get some answers out of him."

Wynter spoke up. "Matthew wasn't supposed to, but I know he emptied his bank at home and brought all the cash he had. He planned to buy some reenactment stuff like Luke's."

"Okay then," Sofia said, "you girls go back to the sutler tents together and keep looking."

After her family had disappeared in opposite directions, Sofia grabbed her phone and scrolled through her contacts. She would never have guessed that one day she'd be glad to have a personal contact at the Cabot Falls Police Station.

Officer Ryan Quimby had gone to the same high school as Sofia. When he answered on the third ring, she identified herself and quickly told him the situation. "Could you possibly come help the police here? They're probably doing what they can, but I'm feeling desperate."

"Come to St. Albans?"

"It's only half an hour away."

"I don't have jurisdiction there, Mrs. Parker."

"I know, but I need your brains, your ability to investigate." Sofia fought back tears and forced the words through a tight throat. "We've searched everywhere. An Amber Alert went out. We don't know what else to do, but the longer he's missing . . ."

The silence on the line seemed to go on forever.

"I'm sorry. Are you busy with an important case?" Sofia asked. She hadn't thought about that.

"You know Cabot Falls. I spend my days answering calls about loose dogs and burglar alarms set off by thunderstorms." He paused, then sighed. "I'll be there within the hour. I'll call you when I arrive."

"Thank you so much." Sofia hung up just as her phone beeped, indicating a low battery. She was running out of time, in more ways than one.

Washington, D.C.
December 1862

Returning from the dead shed, Phoebe pondered her next step. George was disheartened at the news that his friend had disappeared without a trace. It worried Phoebe to see George slip into depression.

After a long day, Phoebe wrote home. She was happy to finally report that their father was improving, if slowly. She wouldn't tell the children that their father was accused of desertion, but she'd sent a private note to Jane a few days before, explaining the situation.

Phoebe closed her eyes for a moment, trying to recall anything entertaining that she could add to her letter. Then she remembered one of the soldiers on Louisa's night rounds who referred to himself as "the earl."

He's best known for how he talks to the other soldiers, Phoebe wrote. *He calls them by their ailments. "How are you, Rheumatiz?" and "Trade apples, Ribs?" and "I say, Nurse A., may I give Typhus here a drink of this?" He's a good sort and makes them laugh, which is appreciated.*

Phoebe then gave the letter to George so he could add a message for John and Annie before she sealed it to post. After George dozed off for a spell, Phoebe stood and stretched, and then went to see if Louisa required assistance. When she'd asked if she could help with non-nursing duties in exchange for the wonderful privilege of having a bed on the nurses' floor, Louisa had snapped up the offer.

Out in the hall, Phoebe was surprised at the commotion coming from the lobby. There was an unusual amount of noise so late in the evening. She hurried down the hall and winced at the sight that met her eyes. Three nurses, three orderlies, and young Marco de Luca were manning a triage and sorting out a group of newly arrived wounded. Some were carried up the stairs to surgery on stretchers. The remaining five were helped into the ballroom to fill empty beds.

Louisa glanced up and spotted Phoebe. "Are you free?"

"Yes. George is asleep for now. What can I do?"

"Two ambulances delivered a dozen men from a skirmish. Spies or scouts or something . . . I didn't catch it all."

"Ambulances?" Phoebe's head snapped up. "Are the drivers still here?"

"No, they've left."

Phoebe could have cried. "What can I do?" she asked, making herself focus on the task at hand.

"Apparently they were fighting in mud. Their faces and hands and clothes are filthy. First things first: I'll clean the wounded areas and bandage them, if you'll come after me and wash them up. Unfortunately the laundress can't bring clean uniforms for them till tomorrow."

Phoebe found a basin of water and clean rags, and she started washing. She was actually grateful to be of help. Being shut up in that tiny back room with her husband was getting claustrophobic. While this wasn't a glorious job, it made her feel useful.

"Wash as fast as you can, Phoebe," Louisa said, handing her a block of brown soap. "Have them take off socks, coats, and shirts, then scrub them well and put on clean shirts until you run out. The attendants will finish them up and put them in bed."

Phoebe forced down her hesitation, clutched her bar of soap, and began. Trying to match Louisa's brisk, cheerful air, she approached her first muddy specimen. He grinned as she surveyed his boots, trousers, socks, and shoes, all encased in mud. Phoebe took heart, pretending it was a normal Saturday night of scrubbing her children. In fact, the youngest two soldiers there were no more than boys. Like sleepy children, they leaned tired heads against her as she worked. One blushed and couldn't look at her while she scrubbed him, talking soothingly.

She had to change the muddy wash water often.

After she finished, an attendant came around with a coffeepot. Although it still smelled vile to Phoebe, she heard more than one grateful comment. "This is bully coffee, ain't it?" one said. He handed his tin cup to Phoebe. "Give us another pull at it, and I'll be obliged to you."

"I'm sorry. It's all gone, but I'll make some more." She hoisted the basin of muddy water. "After I get rid of this."

She poured the muddy water outside the laundry room, then headed to the kitchen to make a pot of what passed for coffee. She rinsed a dirty coffeepot and stepped outside into the cold back garden to dump the water.

The freezing night air took her breath away. The stars and moon glittered off the remaining snow near the building. She had bent to toss the dirty water when movement at the back fence caught her eye.

She peered closely. Who was back there? It looked like Dr. Bertram, who was the most considerate surgeon in their hospital according to Louisa. She opened her mouth to call out to him, then halted in surprise. He was talking quietly to someone on the other side of the fence—a woman.

Phoebe stepped behind a scratchy Juneberry bush and watched Dr. Bertram hand the woman a small package. The woman's face was hidden by her bonnet, but when she turned, Phoebe caught a glimpse. There was something familiar about her face.

Had she interrupted a romantic tryst? Well, if that friendly unmarried doctor had found someone, Phoebe was glad for him.

When the woman turned to leave and glanced up, the moon shone full on her face, and Phoebe suddenly knew who she was. The heart shape with the widow's peak belonged to the nurse from the mansion hospital where James Breckinridge had been.

Hurrying back into the kitchen, Phoebe boiled water for the coffee as she considered her evening. She wasn't in a good position, stationed in her husband's room, to learn anything helpful. If she'd been in the ballroom earlier, she'd have seen the ambulance drivers. Perhaps her husband's attacker had been there that night and she'd missed him.

She needed a way to eavesdrop and snoop around without arousing suspicion. And she must act soon, before the doctors decided George was strong enough to recuperate elsewhere—like jail.

Upstairs that night, she lay awake in her cot, staring at the flickering flames in the fireplace and reviewing what she knew.

George had seen an ambulance driver steal morphine meant for the wounded soldiers, and he'd been shot to cover it up. His only witness, James Breckinridge, had mysteriously disappeared from his hospital and wasn't in the dead shed. Louisa had revealed that morphine was disappearing from the hotel hospital's medicine cupboard, and it was unaccounted for. An ugly thought occurred to her then. Phoebe had seen Dr. Bertram hand a package to a nurse from James's hospital after dark over the back fence. Was the nurse selling morphine the doctor had stolen, and perhaps even stealing it from her own hospital as well?

Phoebe snuggled down beneath her blanket, leaving barely more than her nose out in the cold. Were all the incidents unrelated? It was possible. Or when put together, did they add up to a drug-theft ring much bigger than the ambulance driver? Had her husband merely spotted a minor cog in the whole illegal machine?

Whatever the truth, Phoebe couldn't follow up on anything while she was tucked away in the cubbyhole where George was kept. She had to come up with a reason to be out in the main hospital rooms. She wasn't a trained nurse, so she couldn't do most jobs; newly wounded soldiers who needed cleaning up didn't arrive every day.

She finally drifted to sleep, determined to think of ways to become useful to the nurses.

Phoebe's chance came the very next morning as she descended the stairs, clutching a book she'd borrowed to read to George. At the bottom of the staircase, a young nurse talking to the ward master was nearly in tears.

"But my father's only passing through the city," she explained. "He'll be here just a few hours. He brought me some things from home."

"I'm sorry, Nurse McBride, but we really can't spare you," the ward master said.

"Please. I haven't had a day off in weeks."

"Regardless—"

"Excuse me," Phoebe called, hurrying down the steps. "I'll take her place for a few hours."

The ward master shook his head. "You're not a nurse."

"I've been occasionally helping Nurse Alcott, plus nursing my husband. I've been dressing his wounds and keeping them wet. I can help serve meals, write letters home for the soldiers, things like that."

The ward master frowned at the floor, clearly thinking it over. Finally he looked up. "For three hours only. Can you be back by then?" he asked the nurse.

"Oh yes." The young nurse hugged Phoebe. "Thank you." She vanished before the ward master could change his mind.

Phoebe told George where she'd be that morning, then hurried back to the music room ward where Nurse McBride worked. Determined to keep eyes and ears open for anything suspicious, Phoebe followed orders given by the other nurse and attendants.

Despite having no real nursing duties, she was run off her feet for three solid hours. She now understood why Louisa was against employing convalescents as attendants instead of strong, properly trained men. The recuperating soldiers wanted to help, and they tried, but the feeble men just weren't able to sweep, scrub, lift, and wait upon their sicker comrades for long. The nurses had to step in and help more often than not. As Louisa had complained one night, a dozen women did double duty, and then were blamed for breaking down and getting sick.

After only a few hours, Phoebe was in total agreement. This was only a job for a completely healthy person. Even then, it was exhausting.

Phoebe hated to admit it, but she was relieved when Nurse McBride returned. While she'd attained her goal of working in the main wards to be in the center of the action, the constant demands on her had left no time to observe anything.

However, she had learned one thing.

Phoebe now understood how easy it would be during the rushing madness to steal morphine and pocket it without being seen. It would actually be easier to accomplish during a hectic day with people constantly milling around than during the quiet night when the patients slept.

For all she knew, morphine had disappeared during her short shift that very day.

9

St. Albans, Vermont
Present Day

Sofia couldn't just wait for Officer Quimby to arrive. She wondered what areas she should double-check. None of her family had mentioned the crafters, so she returned to the meadow where they were set up. No one was as observant as old ladies who loved to watch people. Sofia only hoped that the apple doll lady or Amanda Witte, the quilter, was as sharp as the fictional Miss Marple.

The doll crafter and the woodcarver had set out Back Later signs. But as Sofia approached the quilter, Amanda waved and came toward her. Suddenly, she stumbled and fell against the corner of the heavy oak frame. It wobbled and collapsed. Amanda disappeared under it.

Sofia dashed to the quilt frame. "Don't move," she called above the Civil War music blaring from a nearby loudspeaker.

Gritting her teeth, Sofia grasped the corner of the rough-hewn frame and braced herself. As she heaved upward, a splinter pierced her palm, but she barely noticed. Arms quivering, Sofia lifted the beam a few inches off the woman's leg.

"Pull your leg out!" she cried.

Amanda, eyes wide and gray hair poking out of her sunbonnet, scooted back. "Mercy!" She stared up at Sofia, a stunned expression on her face.

Sofia laid the beam firmly back on its corner, then gently lifted the quilter to her feet and settled her in a canvas folding chair.

"Are you all right?" Sofia asked, breathing hard.

Amanda's dimples almost disappeared in her deep wrinkles. "Thank you for rescuing me."

"I'll get some medical help."

"No, I'm fine. Just give me a moment."

Sofia picked the sliver out of her palm. "That frame is heavy."

"My husband used to set it up for me," Amanda said. "Now my friends help." She nodded at the men nearby demonstrating a two-handled crosscut saw. "Have you found your son?"

Sofia told her about her call to Officer Quimby. "He'll have some good ideas of what else to do," she said more confidently than she felt. It was growing more difficult with every passing minute to keep a positive outlook. She moved to leave. "If you're sure you're all right—"

Amanda tried to stand, then fell back heavily. "Ow." She rubbed her leg.

"You did injure yourself, didn't you? I'll go get you some help."

"No no, I'm fine. I'll just rest."

Frustrated, Sofia shifted from one foot to the other. She wanted to leave, but that heavy beam could have easily cracked a bone in the elderly lady's leg.

Amanda was talking about how her family had once been in reenactments with her. ". . . and while I portrayed the famous quilter, my husband represented a Union doctor. Our son and grandson were reenactors too."

"That's nice, but I've got to—"

"We used to set up a tent in the camps, and I cooked all our meals over an open flame." Amanda gestured toward an old maroon van parked under a nearby tree. "Nowadays, I drive home to sleep at night."

"I need to get going—"

"Our son got a job in Alaska and moved away with his family. I haven't seen them in almost three years. My grandson, Joey, looks so much like your boy."

"And I need to keep looking for him," Sofia said firmly.

Amanda took Sofia's hand. "I do so envy you your large family. Enjoy them while they're still at home."

"I will." *Once I get them all home, I may never let them out of my sight again.*

Washington, D.C.
December 1862

After substituting for Nurse McBride, Phoebe was glad to have a quiet evening. She settled George for the night and held his hand till he slept. She realized she must have nodded off when she awoke with a start at a sound in the hallway.

Tiptoeing out, she closed the door behind her and turned to see the most amazing sight. A one-legged phantom was hopping nimbly down the hall toward her. Phoebe recognized the Pennsylvania gentleman she'd read to that morning. It appeared that his fever had taken a turn for the worse. He was balancing himself on one leg, like a meditative stork draped in a white shirt too large for him. A dingy cap sat askew on his shaven head, and he flourished a mug in one hand and an old boot in the other.

"Sir?" Phoebe said, approaching slowly. "What do you have there?"

"My canteen!" he cried, waving the mug. "And my knapsack."

"Let me help you back to bed." Phoebe turned him slowly. How had he hopped out of the music room without being seen? "Come with me."

She took his boot so he could grasp her arm. All the way back to the music room, he gave an animated account of the war, his views on President Lincoln, and his worries about his Enfield rifle.

Before they reached the music room, Nurse McBride came running. "Oh, there you are," she said to the patient. She shushed his talk about the bungled war and incompetent generals and traitors. The nurse helped him back to bed, but Phoebe cringed at his ranting about traitors. Was he referring to George? She gasped. Had he been outside their door because he'd come looking for her husband? *Dear Lord, no!* She hadn't even considered that George might be in danger from the other soldiers.

More anxious than ever, Phoebe checked on her husband to be sure the disturbance hadn't roused him. Despite her exhaustion, she sat by his sleeping form for nearly an hour in case the demented soldier returned. Finally she headed upstairs to her third-floor bed. She was asleep almost before she hit the pillow.

The following morning, she tried to dress quietly so Louisa could sleep, but her friend soon stirred. She leaned up in bed on one elbow while holding the warm blanket up to her chin. "I heard about your delirious visitor last night."

"Yes, poor man. It was sad and a little funny at the same time."

"Just to prepare you . . ."

Phoebe turned from pinning up her hair. "Yes?"

"Before the end of my shift, he died."

"No. I didn't realize he was that bad."

"Nor did Nurse McBride. She was quite upset."

Phoebe remembered the soldier raving about traitors and pointing at her, at the nurse, even at Marco de Luca, passing by in the hall. Were the demented man's accusations unfounded, or were his ravings based on fact? Then she had a terrible thought.

"Was he given morphine to help him sleep?"

Louisa shrugged. "Perhaps, because of his fever."

"Do you think he was given too much? You said overdoses happen."

"They do, yes."

Phoebe turned back to the mirror to finish her hair. Overdoses came in two varieties: accidental and intentional. Was the poor raving soldier "helped" into eternity last night on purpose? If so, why? To stop him from making more accusations? No one would ever know.

He would simply disappear. There wouldn't be a service for him. The men died and were carried away with as little ceremony as on a battlefield. There was nothing she associated with someone passing, like reverence, sorrow, or consolation to those left behind.

At least today was Sunday. A chaplain was coming, and all the able-bodied men would gather in the hotel lobby in as many chairs as the staff could crowd in there. The doors to the wards would be left open so the bedridden might at least hear the singing. George's room was a considerable distance from the lobby, but she hoped it might be loud enough even for him.

Phoebe spent an hour helping two orderlies set up chairs for the service. They all needed inspiration and comfort, even those whose beliefs differed from the chaplain's. And the soothing words of such hymns as *There Is a Happy Land* were bound to lift anyone's spirits.

At ten o'clock the lobby was filled to bursting, with more soldiers standing at the back on crutches. Also attending were as many nurses, orderlies, and officers as could be spared from their immediate duties. Phoebe stood on the bottom step to get a better view.

Louisa had said that the chaplain was a professor from some college. If ever strong, wise, and loving words would do good, it was then. Many faces turned toward the chaplain, full of mute hunger. Phoebe found the sermon rather dry, like a college lecture perhaps, and she longed for words that would stir the men's hearts.

But the instant the hymns started, the lounging figures sat erect. Eager hands reached for hymnals handed out by two drummer boys, and the soldiers broke out with a heartiness that brought tears to Phoebe's eyes. She joined in with enthusiasm. She needed encouragement as badly as they did. She sang with heart through all the verses of *Just As I Am*.

She marveled at the ability of the music to raise spirits right before her eyes. Now she realized why she so often heard songs in the wards: patriotic songs, romantic love songs, comic songs, lullabies, hymns, and anthems. She didn't recall ever hearing a vulgar song, but she imagined if one was started, Louisa squelched it fast in her ward.

Some of the soldiers did not wear their caps on Sunday, though at other times they even wore them in bed. On Sundays, Louisa had told her, many of the men read no novels, swore less, and were more orderly and cheerful.

Phoebe slipped away to check on George, hoping he'd been uplifted by the singing. She wove through the crowded lobby. In the alcove off the hall, she was sorry to see young Marco de Luca in the medicine cupboard. Surgeries didn't stop, even on Sundays, but the doctors could use inspiration and comfort too, considering how many patients died despite their labors.

He was making a note in the log book when she slipped by. When she glanced back, he smiled as he locked the cupboard, but both his hands were empty. He hadn't taken any medicine.

Phoebe smiled back and continued on to George's isolated cubbyhole, recalling Louisa's words about the morphine disappearing. Something nagged at the back of Phoebe's mind, something Louisa had said about how drugs could be stolen. Finally the thought solidified. Louisa had speculated that the numbers in the log book sometimes got lowered *before* anything was actually stolen, so that when the opportunity appeared, the thief could grab it and go.

Could that be what she'd just witnessed? When she left the church service early, had she caught him in the act? Or was her imagination doing something George frequently observed: working overtime?

The peace Phoebe felt after the church service lasted until the next day when the mail was delivered. A letter from Jane and the children—there had been two of them so far—was a joyous event. Jane's news plus the children's drawings and notes were things she treasured. She sat down with George again, anticipating news that would bring them all closer.

But her expectations were dashed with the third line. *Please don't worry,* Jane wrote, *but I felt you should know that Annie's cold has taken a turn for the worse. The doctor says it's not croup yet, and he is keeping a close eye on her. It's her breathing . . . hot compresses . . . medicine in short supply . . .*

Phoebe could swear her heart stopped beating. Annie had always been prone to colds, and even as a baby had suffered with croup. She knew Jane wouldn't worry her unnecessarily. If the doctor was "keeping a close eye on her" when there were so many others sick in the dead of winter, it was probably more serious than Jane had let on.

"I'm sorry," George said, his voice weak. "You'd be home with Annie if it weren't for me."

Phoebe folded the letter. "Don't be silly. Annie's getting wonderful care from Jane and the doctor. She's been through this before."

And each time it gets worse. Coming down with croup in the winter always got harder on Annie. During those times, Phoebe kept a vigil around the clock, listening to her daughter's labored breathing and changing hot compresses on a narrow chest that barely rose before it fell again.

She stared at the tiny framed photograph of the children by the bed. Oh yes, she desperately wanted to be home with Annie.

When she heard the noise of the attendants delivering the noon meal to the wards, Phoebe forced a bright smile for George. "I'm going to find you some bread and broth."

"I'm not hungry."

"You have to eat and get your strength back."

"So I can go to prison?"

"No. So we can prove you're innocent and you can come home to recuperate." She stood up and moved briskly. "No more of that talk. I'll be back with lunch."

In the lobby she encountered Louisa carrying a tray of bandages toward George's room. "I have time while my patients eat," Louisa said, "and your husband's bandages need changing. I don't see many doctors going to your room."

Tears sprang unbidden to Phoebe's eyes. "You're so kind to me. To us." She sniffed, but the tears spilled over, and she quickly brushed them away. "Forgive me."

"What is it? Is he worse today?"

"No." She reached into her apron pocket and produced the letter. "I've heard from home, and our Annie is very sick. She has breathing problems." She clenched her hands into fists. "How I wish I could be in two places at once!"

Louisa gripped her arm and squeezed. "How long ago was the letter written?"

"A week." Phoebe gulped. "She could be much worse by now."

"Or much better. It's just as likely that she's running around and playing this very minute."

"Perhaps." Phoebe smiled. "Jane said they're short of medicine, but that's no surprise."

"Speaking of being short of medicine," Louisa said, "after what your husband saw the driver do, I've been watching the supply of medicines and how fast it's being used. As near as I can tell, every two or three days, a bottle goes missing. Sometimes morphine pills, sometimes liquid, and sometimes laudanum." She paused outside George's door. "I hope there's a good explanation for it. Maybe another hospital requested some when their own supplies ran low."

"Would they come late at night and receive it over the back fence?" Phoebe mused aloud.

Louisa stared at Phoebe as if she'd lost her senses. "What are you talking about?"

Phoebe described the scene she'd witnessed in the back garden. "It was probably a small gift and not drugs at all, but Dr. Bertram gave a package to a woman who is a nurse at the mansion hospital. I saw her there when I was searching for my husband's friend. It was so dark that night, and the woman's bonnet hid half her face, so I'm not absolutely sure it was the same woman."

Louisa nodded thoughtfully, then pushed open George's door and went in, her cheery nurse's voice immediately in place. She kept up her chatter with George as she cleaned his wounds. "You're healing," she said with satisfaction. "I know it's still painful, and it will be as you move more, but you're on the mend."

"How long—?" Phoebe swallowed and forced a smile. "How long before he'll be up and around?"

"Should be fairly soon."

Phoebe felt hollow in the pit of her stomach. That should have been good news, but as soon as George was "up and around," he would be on his way to prison.

Just then, noise erupted somewhere in one of the wards, and Louisa paused in her bandaging to listen. "Phoebe, could you go see if we've been delivered more wounded?"

Phoebe was nearly to the door when it was suddenly flung open. Dr. Kauffmann stood in the doorway, bristling, scowling first at George and then at Louisa. "Nurse, what are you doing?"

"Checking a wound."

"No," he barked, "what are you doing *in here*? Why are you nursing a deserter when our brave boys need you?"

Phoebe gasped, and Louisa froze. "I'm coming, Doctor." She cast an apologetic look at Phoebe and left.

In silence, Phoebe finished wrapping George's leg with the clean bandage, but she couldn't meet her husband's eye.

10

St. Albans, Vermont
Present Day

While waiting to meet Officer Quimby, Sofia revisited the horses' pasture. Although there were several children there asking for rides, Matthew wasn't among them. The actor giving rides hadn't seen him either.

"Have you tried the demonstrations tent?" he asked. Sofia shook her head. "They've got contests for younger boys who impersonate drummer boys and couriers." He lifted a little girl into the saddle. "And behind the food booths in that big open field, they're playing children's games of the period. You know, sack races and the like."

Sofia thanked him and sprinted off, her long skirt flapping around her legs. Matthew wasn't at either place. Fighting tears and despair, she bought a bottle of water and made herself drink it.

Her phone rang then; the caller ID said Ryan Quimby. "I'm in parking lot A, the first one inside the gate," he said. "Where are you?"

Sofia thought fast. "I'll meet you at the old brick hall. Go straight up that hill across from the parking lot. I'll meet you at the front door in five minutes." She hung up and called Jim as she headed for the hall. "Ryan Quimby is here. I asked him to help us look for Matthew."

"Really? That's good of him." Jim cleared his throat. "We just found the tent belonging to the actor who threatened Matthew, but he wasn't around. It's in the Union camp next to the big officers' tent. A man camped nearby said his name is Jacob Clark, but he goes by Jake. He didn't like the guy. We'll keep looking for him."

"Jake Clark," Sofia muttered. She'd give the name to Officer Quimby. Her phone started beeping again. "My battery's low."

"I'll let you go. Just tell Ryan that the actor we talked to said Jake has been in trouble before."

"I'll tell him."

She hung up and power-walked up the hill to the hall. Officer Quimby was already there, but Sofia barely recognized him. Big and tall, with a broad freckled face, he looked more at home in his sports shirt and baseball cap than in his usual policeman's uniform. She quickly filled him in on what Jim had discovered about Jake Clark.

"Let's see what comes up on a background check."

Sofia paced in front of the hall, barely aware of the spectators going in. A few came out with quilt squares and quilt books. It was ten minutes before the officer got the information he'd requested.

Hanging up, he joined Sofia. "Your instincts were right. This character could be trouble."

Sofia's heart skipped a beat and then raced double time. "He has a record?"

"Jake—Jacob Clark—was banned from a previous reenactment for assaulting someone."

"So he makes good on his threats." Despite the heat, Sofia shivered. And Jake even had a rifle. Just because they were supposed to shoot blanks didn't mean he followed orders. And since the guns were period accurate, he also had a bayonet on his. Luke had seen it. "Jim told me where his tent is. Maybe he's back by now."

Moving at a fast clip, Sofia and Officer Quimby headed to the Union camp. A faded Green Mountain Boys flag flew in front of the largest tent. "I think that's the officers' tent, and Jim said Jake's tent was beside it. Jim's still looking for him."

Inside the spacious tent with a table, writing desk, and folding chairs, Officer Quimby showed his police ID and explained his plain clothes. "It's unofficial, but I'm helping in the search as a friend of the family. We were told that one of your men—a Jacob Clark—may have threatened her son this morning before the boy went missing."

The officer, in a coat with shiny brass buttons and polished boots that gleamed, stroked his handlebar mustache. "Jake Clark is a thorn in my side. Right now, he's digging a big hole."

Officer Quimby raised an eyebrow. "Digging a hole? In the park?"

"In the woods behind where the cavalry tie their horses. It's a disciplinary action for firing his weapon in camp, which is strictly prohibited. He claimed he was giving a demonstration for the spectators, but it doesn't matter. It's against the rules, even though we fire blanks. He knew the punishment for firing his weapon."

Sofia had to ask. "But why dig a hole?"

"We try to be authentic during reenactments. It was a common disciplinary practice during the Civil War to have soldiers dig big holes for burying garbage from the camp."

Officer Quimby shook his hand. "Thank you. It's a hot afternoon for digging. Let's hope it makes an impression."

They walked in silence along the row of A-frame tents when Sofia suddenly cried out, "He did it on purpose!" She grabbed the officer's arm. "Jake Clark fired his weapon in camp knowing what the punishment would be."

"And?"

"Why would that show-off want to be exiled to the woods, away from prying eyes, to dig a big hole?" Sofia's fingers dug into Officer Quimby's bare arm. "He's done something to Matthew, just like he threatened. He must have him in the woods, ready to bury him in the hole he has to dig."

"Now, Mrs. Parker, that's highly unlikely," Officer Quimby said, "but let's check. Do you know where the horses are corralled?"

"Follow me."

Dodging groups of reenactors and spectators, Sofia ran through the meadow of crafters, fighting the fear within her. They headed toward the wooded area behind the field roped off for horses.

When *Dixie* stopped blaring over the loudspeaker, the sudden quiet made Sofia aware of a rhythmic *chump, chump, chump.* "It's coming from that direction," she said, pointing.

At the edge of the woods they peered into the shady area under the trees. Sofia could see nothing, but Officer Quimby motioned for her to follow him. Watching the ground for dry sticks that could snap, she moved noiselessly behind the officer through great clumps of red and orange sugar maples and yellow beeches. The trees were thick, trunks blocking her vision more than a few feet ahead.

As the thumping sound grew louder, they approached the edge of a clearing. Circling around one huge trunk, Sofia came face-to-face with the soldier who had to be Jake Clark.

He froze, spade in hand, near a long rectangular hole in the ground. He stared at Sofia, and his dancing eyes seemed to mock her. Sofia breathed hard and fast, the hair on the back of her neck bristling. Clark suddenly raised the spade over his head and shook it at her. Sofia flinched and stepped back, tripping over an exposed tree root, and he laughed. The evil sound chilled her to the bone.

"That's enough." Officer Quimby stepped forward. "What are you burying here?"

"Who wants to know?" He dropped the spade.

With one swift movement, Officer Quimby darted toward the actor, pulling handcuffs from his back pocket. Jake Clark jumped over the hole and raced away from them, crashing into the trees' undergrowth. Officer Quimby sprinted after him, and they both disappeared into the woods.

Sofia dropped to her knees by the half-filled hole. "Matthew!" she cried, clawing at the loose earth with her hands.

In two minutes, she'd uncovered plenty of the camp cooks' garbage, but there was no sign of her son.

Washington, D.C.
December 1862

"It's not your fault," Phoebe said again after Louisa apologized for the third time. "When Dr. Kauffmann found you with George, you had to do what he ordered you to."

"I hated his words, his snarl . . . everything."

It was night, and Phoebe and Louisa were sitting near the fireplace in their third-floor room, sipping cups of very watery tea. They'd reused the tea leaves sent by Louisa's family multiple times, but Phoebe thought it still tasted better than what passed for coffee in the wards.

Phoebe wrapped her fingers around her mug, absorbing the warmth. "George is recovering, and he knows what it means for him." She stared into the fire, mesmerized by the flame. "I have to find the ambulance driver who shot him. For that, I have to be out in the wards when he comes back. I can't spot him tucked back in that closet. He's the traitor, not my husband."

"That driver isn't the only phony among us." Louisa kicked and shoved the long log farther into the fireplace. "One of my soldiers is shamming."

"What's that mean?"

"Once in a great while, I have a soldier who is more healed than he lets on. He's terrified of returning to the fighting, so he pretends to be sicker than he is, or delirious, or unable to walk."

"I can understand that, can't you?" Phoebe asked. "I mean, it's not very brave, but—"

"Yes, but if a doctor discovers it—and they will soon—he can be prosecuted as a deserter. You know what that means." She drained her cup. "Doctors aren't stupid. They've seen this acting before."

"But how is it possible? You can't fake a fever or infection."

"This particular soldier took a bad blow to the head. He stares at the ceiling or straight ahead and doesn't respond when someone speaks to him. But today when the mail arrived, a name similar to his was called. He turned instinctively toward the attendant, but then quickly returned to staring at the ceiling." Louisa leaned forward. "I want to ask you a favor."

"Of course."

"I know this is a painful subject, but I feel that you might be the one to get through to this soldier."

"Me?" Phoebe frowned, but then the light dawned. "Because of George, you mean."

"Yes. The soldier in my ward knows he is facing court martial or execution if he's caught, but maybe you could tell him what the family members go through, the pain it causes, when a loved one is branded a deserter."

Phoebe closed her eyes, took several deep breaths, and reluctantly agreed.

First thing the next morning, after posting a loving note to Annie, Phoebe helped deliver breakfast in the ballroom, and Louisa pointed out the shammer. He looked like a harmless ghost, his skin quite pale. A bushy beard hid the lower part of his face, and his hat brim kept his eyes in shadow, but she could tell he wasn't blinking. Phoebe asked if he wanted some breakfast, but he stared at the ceiling, eyes vacant, body perfectly still.

A young boy no older than her son, one she'd twice played checkers with, called from across the aisle. "He won't answer you, ma'am. He don't talk 'cept in his sleep at night sometimes."

Phoebe perched on the edge of the shammer's cot and lowered her voice to a whisper. "I'm not a nurse," she said, "but I *am* a mother. I know when someone is faking sick because they don't want to go to school." There was no discernible change. "Or get back to their duties."

Phoebe waited. If Louisa hadn't seen him turn toward the sound of his name, Phoebe would never have guessed he was acting. She leaned a fraction closer.

"I'm Mrs. Ashford, and my husband has been falsely accused of being a deserter. You may think you're only taking chances with your own life, but you're not." She studied the unmoving face. "I'm sure you have a mother or wife or sister or sweetheart at home, or a father and brothers. Think of the shame they'll endure—the taunts from others—when you're branded a deserter for pretending to be sicker than you are. The doctors and nurses can tell." Her voice broke. "Don't do that to your family. Don't do it to yourself."

She waited, but there was no response. She began to think that Louisa had misread what she'd seen.

Saddened, Phoebe stood and moved on down the row of beds, giving out the breakfast food—mostly hard bread, a bit of cheese, and "coffee."

"Here's the last of it," she said to a soldier at the end of her short aisle. "I'm afraid your bread is mostly chunks and crumbs."

The gruff-looking man with gray streaking his beard had a surprisingly mild voice. "Thank you, ma'am." Phoebe nodded and tried hard not to stare at his unusual shape. He had very long, very thin, very crooked legs that looked like gray sausages in their tight coverings. His body was short, round in the middle, and he was wrapped up in a big jacket and muffler.

On the way back past the beds with her empty breakfast tray, Phoebe took one last chance. She stopped at the end of the shammer's bed, looked at him staring at the ceiling, and decided to test him.

Leaning close, she whispered, "Shammers are tried and executed as deserters. Executions are reported regularly in the newspaper. So your family will know, and so will the rest of the nation you let down."

Still no response. Phoebe finally straightened and left. "I'm sorry, but there was no response," she said to Louisa as she passed by.

The next morning, Phoebe rose with a heavy heart. It was Christmas Eve, and her family was separated. Black clouds hovered over both George and Annie. She didn't feel like celebrating Christmas any more than the men in the wards did.

As she came down the staircase, she narrowly escaped being run over by the ward master. He strode through the hospital's lobby without acknowledging her and on into the ballroom ward.

"Attention, men!" his voice boomed. "This morning some of you will be released."

Phoebe paused in the doorway to see what he meant.

"I'll call the names of soldiers getting new marching orders this morning." The ward master rattled a sheet of paper. "Some of you are recovered enough to return to your regiments. Some of you go to convalescent homes to make room for someone who needs round-the-clock medical care."

He read a dozen names in a clear baritone voice. Phoebe held her breath, fearful that the shammer had been detected. He stared at the ceiling, one hand twitching at his side. If Louisa hadn't told her differently, Phoebe would have believed he was out of his mind. She hoped that he'd voluntarily make his true condition known, and soon.

The ward master finished, and the shammer's name hadn't been called. "Now look sharp and be ready when the wagons come."

Wagons. Driven by ambulance drivers! Phoebe wasn't going to miss this again.

As soon as the ward master left, there was sudden activity of things being turned upside down and inside out. Boys began to black their boots, those who had them brightened spurs, and knapsacks were overhauled. They'd be ready.

As she turned to leave, the boy she'd played checkers with rushed up to her. "We're off, ma'am, and I'm powerful sorry, for I'd no idea a hospital was such a jolly place."

"I'm sorry you're going too," Phoebe said, her heart aching for how young he was. No wonder some in the press were calling this the Boys' War. In all probability they would never meet again. She knew the boy's mother had died before the war, so she'd tried to make extra time for him when she could. "I've enjoyed our games of checkers."

"It's been like you're my ma. I hope I get another mini-ball somewhere easy, so I'll come back here and you'll take care of me again."

Phoebe pulled him close for a hug to hide the tears that welled up. She hoped fervently that he got through the rest of the war unharmed. If he ever did come back to the Union Hotel, it wouldn't be a hospital and she wouldn't be there.

After explaining her reasons to George, Phoebe found things to do that kept her in the lobby or out on the front porch. She would *not* miss the ambulance drivers this time.

Three wagons showed up midmorning. Phoebe stepped back but kept an excellent view of the front door. The first driver, perhaps in his late thirties, had such a decided limp that Phoebe decided he must be using a wooden leg. He didn't fit George's description of the man who'd shot him.

The second driver was cheerful, flirting with the young nurses and making them laugh. He seemed the right age, but being all bundled up in the cold weather, no bare arms with rattlesnake tattoos were visible. And caps yanked down over cold heads meant she couldn't tell if any were going bald.

The third driver stayed on the front porch. Phoebe overheard a crude joke and caught a whiff of his foul-smelling cigar every time the door opened. She peered at him through a window, but she could see little that was distinctive about him other than a scar on his neck that was shaped like a hook. If one of the three drivers was the would-be assassin—for that's how Phoebe thought of her husband's shooter—her vote was on this man. How could she get him to come inside so she could take him past George's room to be identified?

As she watched while soldiers were moved to the waiting wagons, she realized that the number of people who could smuggle morphine out of the hospital was large: washerwomen taking bedclothes to clean, seamstresses who mended uniforms, anyone delivering food . . . Morphine could even be smuggled out tucked under the deceased being removed.

"I'm leaving now, ma'am." The drummer boy lined up in the lobby to await further orders. Phoebe's heart contracted at his brave smile, and she knew they were both forcing a cheerfulness neither of them felt.

Just then, the driver on the porch stepped inside, the cigar hanging from the corner of his mouth. "Get a move on," he ordered, gesturing to the waiting soldiers. When the drummer waved to Phoebe, he snorted. "Move it, mama's boy, or you're goin' back to the nursery." He shoved the boy, who fell on his damaged knee.

Phoebe gasped and saw the young boy bite his lip hard. But he stood and marched out with rest of the soldiers heading back to their regiments.

Burning to slap the insensitive driver, Phoebe marched up to him. George had said his attacker had a square face, and this man did. "Wait a minute."

He turned, knocking cigar ash on the lobby floor. "Yeah?" His tone was insolent.

Her heart pounded, but she hoped her fear of him didn't show. "Were you near the fighting at Fredericksburg? Did you bring the wounded from that battle?"

"Yeah, me and a hundred other drivers." His black eyes narrowed.

She glanced down, studying his pistol so she could describe it to George.

He followed her gaze and grinned at her. "Is the little lady in need of protection?"

"Should I be?" she asked, her anger boiling over. "Do you plan to shoot *me* in the back?"

"Whoa there." The man stepped back. "You should be in an asylum."

"And you should be in prison," Phoebe shot back.

From out of nowhere, Louisa stepped between them. Phoebe blinked in surprise. *Where did she come from?*

"I need your help," Louisa said firmly, turning Phoebe around. "Immediately."

Without a word, Phoebe let Louisa guide her to the ballroom ward—but not before she saw the cold and calculating look on the driver's face.

11

St. Albans, Vermont
Present Day

Sofia brushed off her dirty hands and dialed Officer Quimby's number. After four rings, it went to voice mail.

"It's Sofia. Please call me when you get a chance. There was only garbage in the hole Jake dug."

While she waited for him to return her call, Sofia decided to try the demonstration tents again, fighting against the feeling that it was useless. Matthew had to be somewhere, but where?

Passing through the meadow, Sofia glanced at Amanda Witte's quilting site and halted abruptly. Wispy hair straggling from her bonnet, Amanda knelt beside a gray-bearded soldier who was propped up against a tree.

Sofia hurried over and squatted beside the Confederate actor. "Can I help?"

Liquid drizzled down the long gray beard that spread across his chest. The actor, his face flushed beet-red, opened his eyes and struggled to speak. Unfocused, he stared vacantly at Sofia; then his eyes crossed and he closed them again.

Amanda waved her reed fan with one hand. "He nearly passed out from the heat," she whispered to Sofia. "I gave him some lemonade, but it didn't help. I have some more here." She tilted the tin cup to the man's lips, but his head fell sideways, and the liquid dribbled onto the grass.

Sofia was anxious to keep hunting for Matthew, but it was obvious that Amanda needed help.

"His wool uniform is too heavy for the heat. Here, help me." Sofia leaned the man forward, braced him, and tugged off his coat. His homespun shirt underneath was soaked with sweat. Pushing his whiskers aside, Sofia unbuttoned the top shirt buttons. A mass of damp gray hairs curled at his neck. "Should I go find a medic?"

"Oh, I don't think so." Amanda fanned the soldier so hard that his hair fluttered in her breeze. "My own husband, God rest his soul, used to feel faint at reenactments in his later years too. It's just the heat—and the excitement."

Sofia gently shook the older man, and he opened one eye. "You should see a doctor."

He smiled crookedly. "Fine in a minute . . . rest here." Rubbing his eyes, he squinted, his eyes crossed and uncrossed, and he blinked. "It's better now. I'm not so dizzy." The old soldier gripped Sofia's arm and rolled onto his knees, but then fell back against the rough tree trunk. "Maybe I'll sit here another minute."

Amanda poured a full cup and helped the elderly man drink most of it, then handed him his tiny round spectacles.

He put them on, then removed them and rubbed them on his shirt. "Darned glasses . . . all blurry . . . can't see at all."

"Now don't you worry," Amanda said. "We're here. Of course, my dear husband used to say something—what was it? About the blind leading the blind . . ." She laughed merrily. "Now isn't that the silliest expression you ever heard? With that arrangement, we'd fall off the edge of the earth."

Sofia resisted the urge to roll her eyes. Was Amanda flirting?

Two women carrying cameras and vinyl folding chairs stopped at the quilting frame. "Excuse me," one called, "do you sell your quilts?"

Amanda glanced over her shoulder. "No, I'm afraid I don't." Joints cracking, she got to her feet and joined them, slipping into her first-person impression. "I'm Jane Stickle from Vermont, and it gets mighty cold come winter. I need all my quilts to keep warm." One woman snapped Amanda's picture. "I quilt to pass the time until my dear husband returns from the war."

Fuming silently, Sofia wished Amanda would get back to the dizzy reenactor. Her heart clamored to keep hunting for Matthew. "Here, have some more lemonade." Sofia raised the cup to the older man's lips, but his handlebar mustache dipped in the drink. Then she tried Officer Quimby's number again. No answer.

Twenty feet away, one of the women studied the intricate piecing of the quilt fastened to the frame. "Quilting might pass the time," she said, "but I'd be bored doing it myself."

"Bored?" Amanda asked indignantly, hands on hips. "Not by a country mile. At quilting parties we exchange current news about the changing political scene. Our quilt names reflect that, like the Lincoln's Platform, Slave Chain, and Underground Railway patterns."

"Come *on*, Amanda," Sofia muttered through gritted teeth as she held the soldier's head upright and steady. *I want to get moving.*

Suddenly the old man's eyes rolled back in his head, showing the whites, and Sofia caught him before he fell over. She followed her instincts and dashed the lemonade in his face.

The soldier coughed and spluttered. "Lie still," Sofia urged him. She waved at Amanda, trying to catch her eye. *I have to leave!*

Sofia called the officer's number again, and this time he answered. "I was about to call you," Officer Quimby said. "I caught Clark and took him to Sergeant Poole. Clark claims that his friends can account for his whereabouts during the time Matthew went missing. They're being tracked down now."

"Please keep me posted," Sofia said, then slipped her phone back into her pocket.

Behind Sofia, Amanda's voice rose over the cannons firing as several more spectators gathered round. "Susan B. Anthony, who believes in equality for the sexes, gave her first talk on equal rights for Yankee women at a church quilting party held in Cleveland, Ohio."

Five minutes later, when the spectators finally moved away and Amanda returned, the older man was resting comfortably, propped up against the tree again. Sofia was relieved to see color back in his face.

She crawled to her feet. "He seems better now," she said. "I need to keep looking for my son."

"Poor Joey." Amanda wrung her hands. "Let me know when you find him."

"Joey?" Sofia tilted her head.

Amanda adjusted her tiny spectacles. "Did I say Joey? I meant Matthew." She stared off in the direction of the booming cannons. "Joey's my handsome grandson—his dad works on the Alaska pipeline." She touched Sofia's arm, a faraway look in her eyes. "I miss Joey. I wish they came home more often."

Sofia squeezed her hand. *I pray that Matthew makes it home at all.*

Washington, D.C.
December 1862

As Phoebe suspected, Louisa had not really needed help when she'd stepped between Phoebe and the ambulance driver. So Phoebe went directly to her husband to describe the drivers.

As she'd feared, she couldn't give him enough specific details for him to confirm that the driver who'd been so unpleasant to her was the same one who'd shot him.

Late that afternoon, a soft knock on George's door was followed by a young nurse popping in. "Hello, I'm new. Nurse Williams, but call me May." She looked no older than eighteen, Phoebe thought, responding to her cheerful grin.

"Hello, May. Nice to meet you."

"I've brought a gift for you." She pulled an envelope from her pocket. "Letter from home, I bet."

"A wonderful Christmas present!" Phoebe cried, noting Jane's familiar handwriting.

Nurse Williams's eyes sparkled with the enthusiasm of someone brand new before the reality of hospital life daunted her. "The ward attendant also had extra bandages, so I'm to change your husband's dressings."

Phoebe was both surprised and touched. "I've kept the bandages wet, so they shouldn't be stuck to his wounds."

"I was told to be quick, so could you lend me a hand?" May asked. "'Many hands make light work,' my grandma says."

Reluctantly, Phoebe put her letter down to read after the nurse left. She was grateful for clean bandages. She'd had nothing new to use since Louisa had been scolded for changing George's bandages; she'd had to tear up her extra petticoat.

Nurse Williams—May—chatted away as she carefully removed the first bandage. She'd come from Pennsylvania, where she'd nursed for six months.

"How is your first day going?" Phoebe asked.

"It's been one excitement after another." She winked. "I've spent many shining hours washing faces, serving rations, and sitting on a very hard chair, with pneumonia on one side, diphtheria on the other, five typhoids in another room, and a dozen dilapidated patriots hopping and lounging about, all staring at the new nurse."

Phoebe laughed. She could well imagine the scene. "Are you nervous caring for typhus patients? I've heard that camp fever spreads fast."

"True, but the men here are clean. It's usually transmitted by lice from an infected soldier, but it takes a week or more. Hopefully we catch all the little critters before they get a chance to spread." She uncovered George's leg wound next. "At least both shots got you on the left side and you have a good right side to lay on. Otherwise, you'd be lying flat on your stomach to heal. How did you get hit like this?"

There was sudden silence. Sofia and George were a frozen tableau.

May's mouth formed a big *O*. "Oh no, you're not . . . ? I mean . . ." Her face flushed a bright pink. "I'm sorry. I didn't know. I thought you were back here for privacy with your wife. But you're the—" She broke off.

"I'm the deserter," George said, bitterness heavy in his voice.

"No you're not!" Phoebe cried. "He's been falsely accused."

"Of course he has," May agreed, hurriedly gathering her supplies. "I'd better get back to the ward."

Quietly and without comment, Phoebe smoothed George's clothing, then covered him and helped him settle back, propped up on his good side.

"Okay, let's hear some good news now," Phoebe said, hoping that that's what the letter held.

But it didn't.

Jane was sorry to write that Annie was worse, and the doctor had called at the house three times. Jane now sat with Annie around the clock.

Phoebe clutched George's hand, and he gripped it tight. "You must go to Annie," he said. "You must. I'm well enough now."

Phoebe searched George's face. It was true that her husband was improving, which would normally mean she could safely head home on the train. But instead, as he healed, he grew closer to being court-martialed and even executed. And without her to protect him, would his shooter try again?

She was running out of time to clear his name, but were they also running out of time with their daughter?

That night, Phoebe spent an hour writing back to Jane. Since she had run out of paper, she turned Jane's letter upside down and wrote between the lines. She thanked Jane profusely for her tender care of Annie in Phoebe's absence.

She didn't say it in so many words, but Phoebe knew Jane would understand how torn she was between her need to be in Washington and her need to be with her daughter. Could anyone truly care for Annie like her own mother? Or, she asked herself, was her desire to be with Annie more for her own sake than her daughter's? *Quite possibly,* she admitted in the privacy of her heart, *but what mother wouldn't feel the same?*

However, she was the only one looking for evidence to clear her husband's good name and save his life, so she must stay. She must have faith in God and trust Jane to do whatever she would do herself if she were there.

After finishing the letter, she handed George the pen. In a bare corner, George added a note, his writing uneven, to tell the children how much he loved them both.

When settling George for the night, Phoebe reached under his head to fluff up the flat feather pillow. "Ow!" she cried, yanking her hand out. The palm of her hand was bleeding. "What's under there?" She lifted the pillow and discovered that Nurse Williams had dropped a pair of very sharp scissors when changing the bandages. Phoebe's cut wasn't deep, but it bled steadily.

Phoebe grabbed a leftover length of clean bandage and pressed it against her palm. She wrapped it around her hand, and then George tied the loose ends together.

"We're a sight, the pair of us," Phoebe said. "I'm here to tend the wounded, not add to the numbers."

She waited until her husband fell asleep and then added a postscript to her letter: *Jane, if Annie's illness is life-threatening, you must tell me. If it is, I'll be on the next train home.*

But first, she'd work to clear her husband's name as if her life depended on it—because *his* did.

12

St. Albans, Vermont
Present Day

Leaving Amanda and the elderly soldier sitting under the tree, Sofia quickly checked the crowded food tents and groups holding barbeques in nearby picnic areas. But Matthew wasn't at any of those places. She knew she should eat something, but she had absolutely no appetite. If—no, *when* they found Matthew, maybe she'd grab some leftover gingerbread from the camper.

Moving away from the food court, she headed toward the sizeable demonstration tent. A sign outside announced "Costumes and Make-Up: Preparing for a Look-Alike Contest." Her breath quickened. That sounded like something Matthew might enjoy. She gasped at the sudden pressure in her chest and had to hold her breath till the spasm passed. He'd been missing for over four hours now.

The huge demonstration tent had two of its sides tied up to let any meager breeze through. Inside, three fans slowly stirred the hot air. Sofia worked her way around folding chairs and benches to walk down the center aisle made of rough-cut boards laid end to end.

Two men dressed as generals Lee and Grant were "debating" the slavery issue for a group of onlookers. Bearded soldiers in uniform and civilians in cooler clothes talked in small groups throughout the tent. Abraham Lincoln and Mary Todd Lincoln were on the raised platform, awaiting their next performance.

Sofia scanned the groups in the tent, and she asked a few

children if they'd seen anyone matching Matthew's description. She had no luck.

Fighting back tears, she dropped onto a bench and closed her eyes. She felt such defeat, such despair. She nearly jumped out of her skin when someone tapped her arm. She shot up with a wild hope that Matthew had found her.

She came face-to-face with Abraham Lincoln.

Actually, it was more like face–to–black coat. Sofia raised her glance upward and encountered the man's warm eyes. If he hadn't won the look-alike contest, she would have been surprised.

"I heard you talking to the children." His voice was deep, his words slow and measured. "My wife and I stroll around the camps all day, and the local police have asked us to keep an eye out for your son."

"Really?" Tears of gratitude welled up. "Thank you. Matthew is only ten. He was supposed to stay with his dad. I mean, my husband was supposed to watch him."

Just then, Mary Todd Lincoln joined them and nodded to Sofia.

"Good luck," Lincoln said, and he moved away with the first lady. Then he stopped, paused, and came back alone. He laid a hand on her shoulder and said, "A house divided against itself cannot stand." He gave a stiff bow and strolled out with Mrs. Lincoln.

Sofia recognized the line from Lincoln's famous speech, and she guessed what he was hinting to her. Nothing good would come from her blaming Jim. A household divided by resentment couldn't pull together, and they needed to do just that. Sofia knew that she and Jim both loved Matthew equally, and she needed to forgive him for letting Mathew go off on his own. And forgive herself for taking her eyes off their son for even a split second.

Lincoln's statement had proved true for their country. The United States—one nation, under God, indivisible—still endured a hundred and fifty years after his famous speech.

Sofia wanted that same quality of endurance for her family.

Washington, D.C.
December 1862

Phoebe left her letter to Jane and the children in the lobby for the mail pickup and then started upstairs to bed. Louisa rushed out of the ballroom and caught her. She whispered so low that Phoebe had to lean close to hear.

"The shammer's time is up," she said. "Dr. Dickerson said they're getting rid of him tomorrow."

"On Christmas Day?" Phoebe's heart sank. "I'll try in the morning to convince him one last time."

Temperatures plunged during the night, and Phoebe was shivering in the ballroom ward the following morning before breakfast was distributed. "A nurse told me you're out of time," Phoebe whispered urgently to the shammer. "You must come clean about your condition. Please believe me. You don't want to be branded a deserter, not for yourself or your family."

He moaned a bit, his eyes closed, and the heavy beard covered his mouth so thickly that if his lips moved, she couldn't tell. Maybe he was feverish after all. Phoebe pushed back his cap and felt his forehead. No, he felt as cool and dry as she did.

He rolled his head from side to side, and she watched closely. Could he truly be "touched in the head," as one soldier had said?

She felt cruel, but if he was actually sane, she had to shock him. "Do you want to be remembered for being a coward?" she whispered. "Do you want your family and friends to hang their heads in shame when your name is mentioned?"

He stopped thrashing and lay still, but remained silent. Phoebe rubbed her cold, stiff hands and waited. She had nothing else to try, nothing at all.

Breakfast trays were being carried in, and a woman filled a basket by the door with a stack of washed and mended uniforms. As cold as George's room was, Phoebe was tempted to grab a pair of those heavy trousers to wear under her skirt. She didn't want to be a thief, but she wouldn't mind being warmer.

Just then, Dr. Dickerson blew into the ward. Phoebe stifled her intense dislike of the man who'd called George a traitor. He started examining the patients deemed ready for release to a convalescent home or back to the battlefield. Soon he was only four beds away.

"You must be honest," Phoebe whispered urgently. "This is your last chance. The doctors are on to you, and this doctor won't be nice."

Three beds away.

Phoebe felt as if she might explode. She knew firsthand how devastated the shammer's family would be if he were accused of being a traitor.

Two beds away.

"Please! Don't do this to your family." Her shoulders sagged in defeat. How could someone actually choose to be branded a traitor? Trembling, she fought tears that welled up and spilled over on her cheeks. She was so very tired, so beaten down.

The doctor was at the bed next to them.

Pull yourself together, Phoebe. She straightened her backbone. She wasn't defeated yet. She'd never give up on George, and she'd done everything she could for the faker beside her.

The shammer continued to stare, unblinking, at the ceiling. Phoebe stood to go, passing Dr. Dickerson as she left.

She had almost reached the door when the doctor barked, "Well, soldier, what's your decision?" Phoebe turned and waited for the shammer's reply. "You're going somewhere today. Where's it going to be?"

Phoebe's breath quickened as the soldier slowly raised an arm and then struggled to sit up. He cleared his throat. "I'll go back to my unit."

She couldn't believe it. Weak with relief, Phoebe blinked back tears of gratitude that he had found the courage to face his fears. She headed down the hall to sit with her husband. Her solace was mixed with the knowledge that the soldier was returning to his regiment, perhaps to be wounded again or even killed. And yet, if he were to die, it would surely be better to die with honor.

Regardless of the outcome, she firmly believed honesty was the best route to take. Integrity sometimes had to be its own reward, for it could be very costly.

At noon that day, after the other patients had been fed, Phoebe went to the kitchen to find something for George to eat. For once he actually seemed hungry, and she took that as a good sign. She stubbornly ignored the scowling cook, his arms crossed over his ample stomach, and soaked some stale bread in a bowl of broth. Phoebe suspected that part of her husband's weakness stemmed from eating so little for days on end. She'd coax him to eat more today.

Rounding a corner, Phoebe nearly collided with Louisa, who was coming out of the cramped staff dining room. After patients were fed, nurses ate at the first ring of a bell.

Louisa threw up her hands in disgust. "It's all gone again."

"What is?"

"The food. The lunch for us."

"Someone stole the nurses' food?" Phoebe asked, astounded.

"No, it was nurses who took it." Phoebe's confusion must have been evident on her face, for Louisa burst out laughing. "I sound crazy, don't I?"

"A little," Phoebe admitted. "What happened?"

"Oh, the usual," Louisa grumbled. "When the first bell rings, there's a stampede to the dining room. Twenty nurses sweep over the table like a swarm of locusts, and there's not a fragment left for any tardy creature who's even fifteen minutes late."

"Were you late today then?"

"No, but before I could get my food, I got called away by Dr. Kauffmann, so I missed my chance to eat. It's impossible to get a drop or crumb after the usual time." She smiled ruefully. "I went dinnerless yesterday too."

"I'll go find you something," Phoebe offered.

"No, the cook is guarding the kitchen like a sentry. Our supplies are late again, and he said he barely has enough for the evening meal." She pulled her shoulders back and adopted her usual cheerful grin. "Just ignore me. I'm not suffering like our poor boys, and fasting is good for the soul, right?"

Phoebe watched her friend and confidante march back to the ballroom. It wasn't right. No nurse should have to bolt her food so fast that it made her sick, just to ensure that she got some. Phoebe couldn't let Louisa go hungry any more than her husband who needed to rebuild his strength; even more people depended on Louisa than on George.

After George ate his lunch, Phoebe reached for her bonnet and string purse. Her remaining cash was low, but if she was careful, she was sure she could find food for them. They'd have their own Christmas feast that night.

She went on foot to the market, bundled against the sudden drop in temperature. Gusting winds made her gasp when the icy air hit her lungs. She trotted to warm up. It wouldn't take long for her toes to go numb. If it was this cold in Washington, Phoebe feared that St. Albans in the north was much worse. She pictured Jane nursing Annie in her upstairs bedroom, the shrieking winds driving sleet against the windows.

With great effort, Phoebe put that image out of her mind and concentrated on finding food. She took a path to the market through the back gardens where washerwomen congregated over steaming tubs. She passed a sad-looking, unkempt cemetery where cedars sighed overhead and dead leaves rustled underfoot. Across from the cemetery, a brook wound like a silver snake past the blackened ruins of someone's house.

When she reached the market, she made careful purchases: a small stock of hardtack crackers, cheese, and apples. All could be enjoyed between official mealtimes, whenever Louisa needed food and whenever George's appetite picked up.

On the way home, deep in thought about Annie's sickness, Phoebe stepped off the board sidewalk and directly into the path of an oncoming wagon. It was nearly on top of her before the driver's shouts penetrated her thoughts.

She glanced up in alarm, then jumped back, her food spilling on the frozen ground. She'd barely missed being trampled by mules and run over by heavy wagon wheels. Her gasping breath made small white puffs in the frigid air. Disgusted, Phoebe noticed that the wagon hadn't even slowed down.

She stared at the backs of the driver and his passenger. Something in her quick glimpse of the driver convinced her that it was the callous driver who'd made fun of the injured drummer boy and pushed him down. As they disappeared around a corner in the direction of the Officer's Hospital, the passenger on the seat turned around. Phoebe gasped. What was kindhearted Dr. Bertram doing with that nasty driver?

Bending to pick up her purchases, she brushed the dirty

apples on her skirt and wiped off the cheese. Fortunately, the crackers had stayed wrapped in her handkerchief.

For the rest of her walk home, she pondered what she'd seen. It could be perfectly innocent. Louisa had told her that Dr. Bertram, their chief surgeon, had refused the higher salary, greater honor, and lower labor of an appointment to the Officer's Hospital. He'd preferred to serve the poor men at the Union Hotel Hospital or return to the battlefront where he had toiled day and night. Surely a man of such moral caliber wouldn't associate with someone who was quite possibly a morphine thief and had shot her husband.

But as much as Louisa admired Dr. Bertram, Phoebe *had* seen him give that woman a package over the back fence late that night. It had seemed clandestine. If there was a legitimate reason for the meeting, surely she would have come to the front door of the hospital in broad daylight.

Phoebe had no answers, but at least she now had some crackers, cheese, and apples to share. That night, George only nibbled a couple of crackers, but Louisa pounced on an apple and cheese like it was manna from heaven.

However, heaven was short-lived. The next day, when Phoebe ran up to their room for more food, the rats had had her cheese for dessert, and the bugs had set up housekeeping in her cracker bag.

"The apples are even gone," she told Louisa grumpily when she returned downstairs.

"Those apples were like all worldly riches," Louisa said, shaking her head sadly. "They sprouted wings and flew away."

Phoebe tried to match Louisa's accepting attitude, but it was harder than she let on. She had so little money left, she was no closer to clearing her husband of desertion charges, and their little Annie was suffering at home, with neither parent to comfort her. Phoebe knew the vanished food was a small thing by comparison, but sharing an apple with Louisa at the end of the day would have been a comfort.

13

St. Albans, Vermont
Present Day

Outside the demonstration tent, Sofia watched President and Mrs. Lincoln stroll toward the shaded lane where regiments from both sides were already lining up. Enthusiasm ran high in the crowd as they prepared for the last battle of the day. Sofia felt insulated and removed from the excitement—almost invisible.

Thinking her headache might lessen if she ate something, Sofia circled the base of the hill toward where she'd parked the camper. The girls had taken the leftovers there. Since there were no windows in the back of the camper, she'd take an extra five minutes and change into something more comfortable. She wished now that she'd brought shorts, given how unseasonably warm the day had turned out to be. Still, jeans would be an improvement over a long skirt entangling her legs.

She wove in and out of the crowds on autopilot, barely aware of her surroundings. Her fear-induced mental numbness made it hard to think or even feel.

By the time Sofia reached the parking lot, sweat was running down between her shoulder blades. She worked and wiggled the key in the small door at the back of the camper. *Finicky is right*, she thought. After excessive fiddling, she finally popped it open. She hitched up her skirt and stepped inside, leaving the key in the lock since she would be just inside.

The first cooler was empty and the second one held only half a tray of lemon cakes, but she hit the jackpot with the third cooler, where she found two raspberry-filled tarts. She popped a bite of tart into her mouth, then rooted around behind the coolers for her gym bag. It sat on top of Marla's extra firewood, a spare tire, and a couple of fishing rods. Sofia pulled the back door nearly closed so she would have a bit of light, then crawled deeper into the camper and collapsed onto a faded seat cushion. She sneezed at the dust that billowed up.

She had nearly finished changing when an explosive blast made Sofia jump and crack her head on the side of the camper. She groaned as another round of cannons thundered in the distance. "What in the world?" she muttered, rubbing her head. It wasn't time for the battle yet. The troops must be warming up, as they had for the first demonstration of the day.

With the afternoon sun beating down on the tin roof, the camper was turning into an oven. Sweat trickled down her scalp and on down the back of her neck. *With no ventilation, a person could roast in here!* She was determined to finish changing quickly and get back outside. Rebel yells and additional rounds of rapid gunfire echoed down to the parking lot.

Then, with another loud bang that sounded much too close for comfort, the camper was plunged into total darkness.

Sofia stifled a scream, realizing that the bang had been the door slamming shut. Bent double, she stumbled to the small back door and twisted the knob.

It wouldn't budge.

"Come on." Sofia shoved at it with her shoulder, but it was stuck fast. How had that happened? There wasn't enough wind to have slammed the door that hard. As she jerked and twisted the knob, she finally admitted it.

She was trapped.

The bitter taste of panic rose in her throat.

"Breathe deeply," she instructed herself. "Calm down."

Sofia tried the stubborn door one more time. When it still wouldn't open, she sat down and gave it several hard kicks. This felt like more than a finicky lock.

What was going on? Was the door blocked somehow?

Was it some mischief-maker's idea of a practical joke as he sauntered through the parking lot? Or was one of Jake Clark's friends trying to scare her?

She scrambled back to where she'd tossed her calico skirt and grabbed her phone from her pocket. She'd call Officer Quimby to come get her out. She pressed buttons and shook the phone, but it didn't respond. Then she remembered how many times she'd heard it beeping earlier in the day, warning her of a low battery.

Only now it wasn't low. It was dead.

Washington, D.C.
December 1862

What a low-down trick, Phoebe thought, *stealing the apples, especially since I nearly died getting them.* Where had Dr. Bertram been going so urgently anyway when she'd nearly been run down? She'd ask him if she found a chance. While most of the nurses were afraid to question the doctors, she wasn't. She didn't have to work with them, and she wouldn't leave any stone unturned to save her husband from execution—even if it meant cross-examining the good doctor.

She had her chance later that afternoon when she spotted him in the lobby. But as she stepped forward, he veered down the adjoining hallway toward the alcove holding the medicine cupboard. Phoebe changed course, pulling back to watch. While he had every right to be there, her instincts told her that the medicine cupboard was her key to finding answers.

Dr. Bertram whistled while he unlocked the cupboard. In no apparent hurry, he wrote in the notebook. Louisa said they always changed the number to reflect the medicine taken and marked down which kind. Phoebe had to admit that Dr. Bertram didn't act the least bit sly or duplicitous.

But just the same, she continued to watch. He finished writing, glanced over his shoulder, and paused. Holding her breath, Phoebe drew back into a doorway while still keeping a clear view of the doctor. She didn't even dare to blink.

But what he did next was totally unexpected. He reached into the pocket of his white coat and removed a brown glass bottle. Continuing to whistle nonchalantly, he reached toward the back of the cupboard. His hand came out empty. Then he carefully locked the cupboard and strolled back the way he had come.

Bewildered, Phoebe frowned and shook her head. *What was that all about?*

Why put medicine back? Had Dr. Bertram taken more pain-killers than he needed for an earlier surgery? Was he returning the unused bottle? Why wouldn't he leave it in the operating room for the next surgery? Or . . .

Her heart skipped a beat then. Had he instead taken a bottle of morphine pills earlier, poured them into something else, and was now returning the empty bottle? He had reached toward the back of the cupboard. An empty bottle wouldn't be noticed back there, especially through brown glass. When the ward master did inventory, the actual number of medicine bottles would be correct.

Ignoring a nagging headache that was growing stronger, Phoebe stopped by the ballroom to tell Louisa what she'd seen, but the nurse was busy cleaning and re-dressing wounds.

"Sorry," she said, "but I won't be free to talk for a good while."

"Later then," Phoebe said.

Turning to leave, she spotted a new young boy set apart from the others, and her heart caught in her throat. Each boy who arrived at the hospital made her miss her son, John, even more. Yet the young drummer boys and couriers also reminded her to be grateful that John hadn't run away to enlist with George, though he missed his father dreadfully. He'd felt it his duty to stay home and take care of his mother and sister.

Sweat soaked the boy's matted and unkempt brown hair. She leaned down and felt his forehead. He was burning up and obviously weak. Maybe he could eat a bit. She reached into her skirt pocket for a cracker salvaged from the bugs. "Are you hungry?" she asked gently, holding the cracker to his lips. He didn't make a move to bite.

Louisa walked by then with a pile of soiled bandages. "Poor little boy," she said over Phoebe's shoulder.

"What's wrong with him?" Phoebe whispered, following Louisa a few steps away. "I don't see an injury."

"No injury. It's typhoid fever. It's why he's separated from the rest."

"He feels terribly hot."

"The fever will climb higher still. He'll break out in rose-colored spots soon."

Phoebe glanced back at him. "He's so malnourished, but he wouldn't even open his mouth for a bit of cracker."

"I know. Loss of appetite is normal for typhus, along with a dry mouth and furred tongue."

Phoebe wondered about the boy's mother. Was she waiting at

home, desperate for news, wondering why his letters had stopped? "How did he contract it?"

"They get it in camp." Louisa dropped her soiled bandages in a basket and reached for the stack of clean ones. "They're crammed in together, sharing infected bandages and contaminated water."

Phoebe shuddered and lowered her voice even further. "Will he make it?"

"He has a good chance," Louisa said, "but one out of three with the disease die from it."

Louisa had to get back to work, and Phoebe headed upstairs to lie down briefly. Her headache had escalated, and she hoped to ease it. First she checked her palm to clean the cut. It was tender and reddish. *Quite normal*, she reassured herself. The redness looked like her husband's wounds, but her cut was minor compared to George's injuries.

Leaving her shoes on, she lay down and pulled a blanket up over her shoulders. When she woke up later, Phoebe was dismayed to find her headache much worse. The mattress felt hard as a board, and she felt as stiff as one herself. She sat motionless on the bed and winced at the pounding in her head. Then, pulling her shoulders back, she made her way downstairs to George. Coming around the corner, she noticed someone in the medicine cupboard.

It was the young medical student. He wrote in the book, grabbed two bottles, and then turned and spotted Phoebe.

"*Ciao*," he said. "How is your *bambina*? She is nine, no?"

Phoebe smiled despite her pounding head. "How did you remember that?"

"I have little sister in Italy," he said. "Isabelle—Izzy—has nine years also."

"Annie's sickness is worse," Phoebe said, a catch in her throat. "I'm hoping for good news soon though."

"Is *difficile*, no?" Marco closed the cupboard. "I hope for good report to you *rapidamente*—quickly."

"Thank you." Phoebe watched as he strode down the hallway and started up the staircase, acutely aware that he'd neglected to relock the cupboard.

She could have reminded him, but this was her chance to see the notebook containing the medicine records. For one thing, she was eager to see what Dr. Bertram had written when he put the bottle back. Louisa said the doctors had to sign their names and the date, write down which drug they were taking and how much, then lower the number to reflect how much painkiller was still available so the ward master knew when to requisition more.

This was her chance to see those records—the chance she'd been waiting for. If she could note which days the inventory dropped and which days the drivers picked up patients, she could see how often the dates matched. Surely the notebook was the key to finding such patterns.

She waited in the alcove until there was a lull in the foot traffic through the lobby. Heart in her throat, she grabbed her chance. She opened the cupboard, snatched the notebook, and flipped quickly through several pages. Frowning, she studied the entries, most of which resembled glorified chicken scratches. She couldn't make sense of the scribbles without sufficient time to study them. She tried to remember exact dates when that nasty driver had come to the hospital—the one she suspected had shot George. She would bet her bottom dollar that those days would also show a marked drop in the inventory. A drop not explained by the number of surgeries.

Footsteps were heading down the hallway, coming closer. Phoebe panicked and froze. She couldn't take the book—its disappearance would be noticed immediately—so in desperation, she tore two pages from the previous week's record and stuffed them into her apron pocket. She closed the cupboard door with a click.

Phoebe turned to find Marco de Luca coming toward her, a quizzical look on his handsome dark face. Had he seen her in the cupboard or stuffing papers into her pocket?

He took a key from his pocket. "Mrs. Ashford, I do it again, no? I forget to lock the cupboard," he explained. "Dr. Bertram tells me again." He locked it with a quick twist of the skeleton key, then peered closely at her. "You are *malato*? Sick?"

Phoebe could well imagine that she looked ill. She felt very near to fainting from fright. "I, uh, my headache is worse, that's all."

"You will lie down, *resto*?"

"Yes, I will rest," she agreed, willing him to leave.

"I take your arm," he said, "before you faint."

Although Phoebe had intended to visit George when the medical student returned to the surgery, she let him help her up to the third floor. "Thank you, Dr. de Luca," she said. "You are very kind."

"I am Marco, remember? You must nurse yourself," he said, smiling. "Your *marito*, er, husband, needs you in health, no?"

Phoebe nodded, thanked him again, and closed the door to Louisa's room. She hurried to her bed, not to lie down, but to hide the papers torn from the drug notebook beneath her hard mattress. She'd show them to Louisa later, but in the meantime, she couldn't be caught with them on her or accidentally have the papers fall out of her pocket.

After ten minutes, she opened the door a crack and peered out. Head throbbing, she steeled herself and descended the stairs to the lobby, clutching the banister the entire time.

14

St. Albans, Vermont
Present Day

$\mathcal{S}$ofia shook her throbbing head. *My phone can't be dead. Not now.*

As the temperature in the camper rose steadily, sweat trickled down Sofia's face and neck. She beat her fists repeatedly on the metal camper door, screaming, "Help me! Please, someone, help!"

When no one came to her rescue, she groped around, found a tire iron, and pounded again, oblivious to the dents she inflicted on the door. Still no response. Her pounding blended seamlessly with the barrage of rifle fire and exploding cannons from the battlefield.

How long would the battle last and drown out her cries for help? How long could she survive in this oven?

Breathing hard, Sofia was terrified that she'd suffocate if she didn't escape soon. Most spectators were clear around the other side of the hill, watching a battle that might continue for an hour. How could she break out? The only bit of gray light seeping into the camper's dark interior came from the tiny sliding window that opened into the pickup's cab. Sofia slid open the rectangular window, only to be blasted by even hotter, more-suffocating air from the cab.

Couldn't they have made this window bigger? she thought irritably. Then she could crawl through to the cab and escape out the driver's door.

The cannons continued their bombardment, with bursts of rapid gunfire at short intervals. In desperation, Sofia again kicked and pounded on the back door. No one responded. The deafening volume of the battle drowned out her efforts.

Sinking to the dusty floor of the camper, Sofia gasped for air. She might as well face facts. She was trapped in a tiny metal box, about to be cooked alive in the hot afternoon sun.

As she sat, the cannons booming in the distance fused with the thundering in Sofia's head until they were one and the same. She was running out of time. And what about Matthew? He'd disappeared five hours ago. When another round of pounding and screaming brought no help, her knees buckled, and she collapsed onto the cushions. She was so very thirsty. She now regretted that there'd been no leftover lemonade.

Wait. Ice. Sofia crawled to a cooler and got a handful of melting ice chunks. She sucked on one and rubbed others on her forehead and neck. She sighed with delight as melting ice mixed with the sweat.

She rolled over and something jabbed the back of her leg. She peered through the gloom and felt around. It was a fishing pole.

She scrambled up, grabbed the pole, and poked it, handle first, through the tiny sliding window into the cab. She stretched her arm, her shoulder cramping as she pressed her face against the window. She tapped the pole on the horn on the steering wheel. First it barely squeaked, but then, with more pressure, a short, loud blast filled the air.

"All right!" Sofia yelled, honking the horn over and over. She hoped it sounded like a car alarm and would bring someone running.

Her triumph slowly faded, though. She kept it up for five minutes, but not a single soul checked out the noise in the parking lot. The guns and cannons apparently drowned out her honking too.

Sinking to her knees, she struggled to drag hot, heavy air into her tired lungs. She admitted temporary defeat. Her honking wouldn't be noticed until the battle was over. She would make another attempt then.

"If I live that long," she whispered.

Washington, D.C.
December 1862

Phoebe debated long and hard, but she decided not to tell George about the pages she'd torn from the drug notebook. She might not find anything of value there, and she didn't want to raise his hopes just to dash them.

As the evening wore on, she struggled to remain upright in her straight-backed chair as she read to her husband from *The Daily Evening Star.* George was unusually quiet, barely stirring, and not at all hungry. She tried not to fuss too much, but he seemed to be relapsing. He shivered violently sometimes, and Phoebe again laid her coat over his quilt for extra warmth.

It was difficult to find interesting bits to read that had nothing to do with the war or reminders that they were far from home on Christmas, and her headache made the reading harder. Phoebe knew she was shivering more than could be accounted for by the frigid room.

She was massaging her chafed hands when Louisa opened their door. "Phoebe, come quickly."

"What is it?" She stood up too fast, swayed a moment, and then joined Louisa in the hall.

Disappointment—or sorrow—clouded Louisa's face. "A moment ago, after being in the medicine cupboard, Dr. Bertram stepped out back again with another package."

Phoebe didn't blame her friend for feeling disillusioned. No nurse would want to believe that their most charitable surgeon was making money by selling medicine—drugs that the wounded desperately needed. But privately, Phoebe hoped it was true. She was desperate for a break. "Thank you for telling me."

"I must get back to my ward. A delirious soldier is making enough racket to wake the dead, and I just got them settled." Louisa gripped Phoebe's wrist. "Be careful."

Phoebe hurried into the kitchen. It was empty, but a candle lantern burned on the worktable. Leaning over the opening at the top, she blew it out. She didn't want any light spilling out when she opened the back door.

Slipping outside, she left the door open an inch and found her hiding spot behind the Juneberry bushes. There was less moonlight than last time, and she peered through bare branches at the two outlined forms at the back fence. One was Dr. Bertram, according to Louisa. The other outline definitely belonged to a woman. While the bonnet hid her face, this time her voice was clear.

It was definitely the nurse from the hospital where James Breckinridge had mysteriously disappeared.

What was the woman doing with the drugs? For surely that was what Dr. Bertram had taken from the cupboard. Phoebe couldn't imagine any reason that wasn't illegal. If their meetings were only medical professionals sharing medicine, why hold them in the dark over the backyard fence?

Phoebe held her breath to hear them better, but their voices had dropped. She shivered until her teeth chattered, and she wished she'd grabbed her coat. A wave of dizziness passed over her, and she leaned back against the wall.

When the light-headedness passed, she straightened in time to see the two shadows come together briefly, then pull apart. The woman slipped down the alley in silence, and Dr. Bertram hurried inside the kitchen, passing within three feet of where Phoebe hid. He closed the door with a thud.

This is my chance.

Phoebe knew the streets of Washington were dangerous for women at night, especially if they were alone. Did that woman have a carriage parked around the corner? She had to find out where the drugs were being taken. It would help prove morphine thefts were happening, just as George had said. Since his only witness, James Breckinridge, had either died or disappeared, this could be her one opening to discover the truth. Otherwise, George would remain falsely accused—and then either branded or executed for desertion.

The woman was soon swallowed up in the shadows. Phoebe had to follow her. There was no time to go back for her coat or to tell Louisa what she planned.

Phoebe picked her way to the fence through crunchy dead leaves and frozen mud ruts. Following along the pickets, her fingers found the gate opening. She lifted the iron latch, eased open the squeaky gate, and stepped out into the alley.

The woman's outline with its flowing cape and bonnet was all Phoebe could see. She counted to ten after the woman disappeared around the street corner. Then she ran, slipping where the cobblestones were covered with frost and old snow.

At the crossroads, she peered around the corner of an empty brick store. The woman in the voluminous cloak moved swiftly on the deserted street. She never glanced back, making it easy for Phoebe to follow. And since there was a partial moon, the city hadn't turned on the streetlights. The nurse was heading in the general direction of her own hospital, but surely she couldn't walk all that way. It was too cold and much too unsafe. Still, Phoebe didn't see a carriage anywhere.

Shivering despite her speed and heavy skirt, Phoebe slowly closed the distance between them. Abruptly, in the blink of an eye, the woman disappeared.

Phoebe peered through the darkness. She'd been there one moment and vanished the next. Where had she gone? Had she ducked into an entryway to get out of the wind? Or stepped between two buildings? Phoebe slowed, staring ahead intently. She was so focused on the distance that she stumbled and tripped over something at her feet.

"Get out of here," a voice growled from the shadows, "or you'll be sorry."

Crying aloud in horror, Phoebe hoisted her skirts and ran. Glancing over her shoulder to be sure she wasn't followed, she spotted a large lump—or maybe it was two smaller ones—in the doorway of Landsburgh's Department Store. Her heart pounded as she peered anxiously into other shadowy doorways she passed. How many more dark doorways were hiding homeless men?

What am I doing? she wondered suddenly. Had she taken leave of her senses? She had two children to think of.

And yet, if she didn't trail the woman, she had no other clues to follow, no further ideas to clear George's name. Grimly, she pulled her shawl even more tightly around her shoulders. What she would give for her winter coat right now!

She raced toward the point where she'd last spotted the woman. At first she made out nothing in the foggy mist that was moving in from the river. But then a form materialized from the shadows ahead, almost appearing to float, and passed by a hotel where light spilled onto the road.

It was the nurse.

But as Phoebe closed the distance between them, the woman

turned yet another corner—taking her in a direction away from the mansion hospital. Was she going home? Or . . . Phoebe's eyes widened. *Wait.* This was the way she'd come from the train station her first night in Washington. This street had taken her past the White House.

Skirts held up, she ran for the corner, slipping and sliding on invisible patches of ice. She reached the side street in time to see a small black carriage drive away. Was the nurse inside? The *clop-clop* of horses' hooves on cobblestones soon faded into the darkness.

Defeated and shivering violently, Phoebe fought tears as she turned back toward the hotel hospital. She'd been *so close.*

Mentally she counted the blocks back that she had to cover. Five or six anyway, and no one was on the street who could help her. Starting back, Phoebe noticed things she had missed when she'd been focused on following the nurse. This particular street held several very large mansions with vacant lots between. Many homes still had candles burning in downstairs rooms. How many of them had been turned into hospitals? Could the nurse have disappeared not into the carriage, but into one of them? She hadn't actually seen the woman get into the carriage. Perhaps the nurse was visiting a private citizen, or the home of a surgeon who couldn't tend the wounded night and day without the help of painkillers.

Stamping her feet to restore circulation, Phoebe shivered violently as she walked. When running after the woman, the wind had been at her back, but now it blew full in her face. Without her bonnet, her hair came loose and whipped across her eyes. She pulled her shawl up around her head and covered her face. She had to pick up her pace. While her husband might still be asleep and not miss her, Louisa was another story. If she found Phoebe absent, she'd be worried sick, especially after Phoebe had told her about the illicit meeting.

Phoebe crossed the street away from the doorways where the homeless men slept. She constantly checked over her shoulder to make sure she wasn't followed. It now dawned on her what a foolhardy—and dangerous—thing she had done, following that woman into the dark streets of Washington, D.C.

15

St. Albans, Vermont
Present Day

As the battle raged on outside, Sofia sat huddled inside the dark camper, her mind racing. *Where is Matthew? How will I get out of here?*

She drifted in and out of a foggy sleep. One tidbit of information would surface, and then another, but she couldn't fit them together. Something flitted around in the back of her mind. She was getting as confused as Amanda, mixing up past and present. That sweet woman had sounded so lonely when she'd talked of losing her husband, then of her son and grandson moving away. What was it she'd said about Matthew? That he looked just like her grandson, Joey. Sofia frowned. There was something else, but it eluded her. She tried to concentrate, but the heat and the noise made it so difficult.

Then she remembered.

Sofia had watched Matthew race down the hill toward the battlefield, and shortly afterward, Amanda had hurried away too, heading in the same direction. Had she been following Matthew? Surely not. Most of the reenactment activities were down there.

But if she had been tailing Matthew, why? And where was Matthew now if she'd caught up with him?

An image of Amanda's maroon van parked under the trees popped into Phoebe's mind. It was an old VW with tinted windows in the back, used for hauling her quilting frame. Could she have lured Matthew inside there somehow? *No.* If she'd tried to lock him in there, Matthew would have made more racket than a caged gorilla.

That is, if he could make noise. If he was conscious.

She tried to piece things together, but she slipped into unconsciousness in the middle of a thought, only to awaken moments later, gasping for breath. Surely the battle was nearly over. Dizzy and faint, Sofia finished the last bits of ice in the cooler. She'd be desperate for water soon.

Dizzy. Groggy. What did that remind her of? Frowning, she struggled to remember. The older man, the reenactor who portrayed a surgeon. He'd been sluggish and faint, but Amanda had been so solicitous, giving him some of her own lemonade.

Or . . . had the lemonade *caused* the old man to faint? Had he been drugged?

Sofia tried frantically to follow that train of thought. Had she drugged Matthew too? Had he been asleep in her van all this time?

Her eyelids drooped, and her head fell forward, then snapped back. She had to stay awake. Yet she must have nodded off because she suddenly awoke with a jolt, aware that something was different. What was it? Then she knew—the silence.

The battle reenactment was over.

Gripping the metal sides of the camper for support, Sofia's legs quivered as she crawled to her knees. With her last ounce of strength, she shoved the fishing rod through the camper window again and pressed on the horn. She'd only honked half a dozen times when a curious face appeared at the driver's-side window.

Hands cupped around his eyes, the sunburned man peered into the cab. "Anyone in there?" he called.

"Yes. Back here!" Sofia screamed hoarsely. "I'm trapped in the camper!"

The man blinked in surprise when he caught sight of Sofia's face at the tiny window. A moment later, after the man had no luck wiggling the key Sofia had left in the lock, he yanked on the door until it popped open.

Sofia lurched forward, stumbled, and fell out the door. She landed on the gravel, where small rocks pierced her hands. Eyes closed against the blinding light, she gulped cooler air into her lungs.

The man reached down, his sun visor falling over his eyes. Supporting Sofia's elbow, he helped her to her feet. "Are you all right, ma'am?"

Faint and trembling, Sofia nodded, her throat too parched to talk. She perched on the bumper, and the man handed her a nearly empty soda can.

"Here. It's not much, but it's wet. Drink this."

Sofia's hands shook as she raised the can to her mouth, and half the liquid spilled down her shirt. Still, nothing had ever tasted so good to her as that flat, lukewarm soda.

Sofia shook the man's hand. "Thank you. I'm sure glad you came along."

"Me too." He wiggled the knob. "You must've slammed the door too hard and it jammed," he said. "These old locks will do that."

"Maybe," Sofia agreed, but she knew that she hadn't even latched the door, much less slammed it. Someone else had done that for her. "Thank you so much. You may have saved my life."

"Glad I could help." The tourist nodded and left. Her harsh breathing slowly evened out as she studied the parking lot. Was locking her in some kid's idea of a practical joke? Or was someone doing a good deed by closing the door, not knowing someone was inside? Or had that innocent-looking little quilter, Amanda Witte, followed her to the parking lot and locked her in? If so, why?

Sofia knew the answer as soon as the question entered her mind. Amanda wanted time to get away before Sofia found Matthew in her van.

She took off, stumbling at first, then finally running. *Why'd my phone have to die?* She should have borrowed her rescuer's phone and called Officer Quimby. But if her phone was dead, she couldn't access her contacts, and she didn't recall the officer's number.

There was no time to go looking for Sergeant Poole or any other police help. She'd have to handle Amanda on her own.

Washington, D.C.
December 1862

Frozen and feeling fragile, Phoebe made it back to the hospital before midnight. It took three cups of hot weak tea and an hour by the fire before she thawed out.

The following five days were anticlimactic, as neither Phoebe nor Louisa spotted any more drug disappearances or clandestine meetings over the back fence. Phoebe studied the stolen pages from the log book, but she couldn't tell whether there were discrepancies.

Other thoughts had consumed Phoebe during those days. She hadn't heard from Jane all week. Had Annie grown worse? If so, why hadn't Jane written as Phoebe had begged? Had Jane's letter gone astray? Louisa reminded Phoebe daily that mail during wartime could be sporadic. While Phoebe had received James Breckinridge's letter in just a few days, letters for the wounded were often weeks old when they arrived. To the railroads, moving troops and supplies outranked moving the mail.

Phoebe knew that was true, but she couldn't stop the thoughts that assaulted her. Had Annie grown much worse—or even died—and Jane couldn't bring herself to write and tell her?

For no apparent reason, both Phoebe's and George's fevers escalated. Phoebe could barely stand the pounding in her head at times, and neither of them had an appetite.

"At least it saves on food," she'd joked to Louisa, trying to make light of her affliction. Surrounded in the hospital by the worst suffering she'd ever seen, Phoebe felt selfish to even mention it.

"This can't go on," Louisa told her one night. "I can see that you're miserable." She joined Phoebe, who was wrapped in a blanket by the fireplace. Her cool hand touched Phoebe's forehead, then the back of her neck. "You're burning up."

"It's not serious." Phoebe forced a smile, but her lips quivered over her chattering teeth. "The boys downstairs deserve your tender mercies far more than I do."

"That may be, but you won't be any good to George if you keel over." She ran a practiced eye over Phoebe.

After Louisa left, Phoebe huddled deeper inside her blanket. She felt sicker than she'd ever been in her life.

Later that day, Dr. Bertram appeared in George's room while Phoebe was reading to him.

"Nurse Alcott is concerned about you two," he explained. "I'd like to examine you." Within fifteen minutes he'd made his diagnosis.

Phoebe and George had both contracted typhus.

Shivering, Phoebe gazed at George in despair. *Typhus.*

Dr. Bertram rubbed the back of his neck. "I don't understand how this happened. You're both isolated back here. You shouldn't have picked up anything in quarantine like this."

Phoebe frowned, trying to focus on his words, when something occurred to her. "Oh, doctor, I think I gave this disease to George!"

"How?"

"I touched a young boy about a week ago who had it."

"But Nurse Alcott tells me she instructed you in proper handwashing. She said you follow it religiously."

"Yes, I'm very careful."

"Then you didn't cause this, Mrs. Ashford." The doctor paced the width of the tiny room in four steps, then turned back to her. "You see, it takes a week or ten days to develop symptoms. Something else must have occurred about that long ago."

"I don't know what it could be." Phoebe swallowed hard. "Are you sure it's typhus?"

"It appears so. If it's truly typhus, there will be severe headaches, a sustained high fever, and a cough. A rash may appear too." His shoulders slumped, and his weariness showed. "Marks of typhus include severe muscle pain, chills, lethargy, and sensitivity to light."

Phoebe's eyes opened wide in alarm. "I haven't been coughing much, but George has. And we both have most of the other symptoms." She sprang up, then wove dangerously on her feet.

Dr. Bertram caught her around the waist and eased her back into her chair. "Sit. Please. You're a very sick woman."

Phoebe stared at George's utterly still form. He was worse than lethargic today. It was more like being in a coma. She gripped the doctor's hand as if it were her lifeline. "What happens next, doctor?"

"Hopefully you will fight it off."

"And if we don't?"

The doctor hesitated. "Becoming delirious means it's worsening, but hopefully you won't reach that stage."

"But if we do, what's after that? I need to know what to look for."

"Mrs. Ashford . . ."

She waited, bracing herself, her eyes never leaving his face.

"Death is the final symptom," he said, "if you can call it that." He swallowed hard as his eyes went back to George. Then he bent over and peered closely at George's bandages, touching and examining them. "Where did you get these?" he asked. "We don't use this kind. The material isn't absorbent enough."

Phoebe thought back. "It was that new nurse, May something. She used them when she changed his dressing."

"I must ask her how these came into her possession."

"An orderly gave them to her, she said. I was very grateful. George hasn't had much medical attention."

Dr. Bertram had the grace to look embarrassed, but he only said, "You are to go upstairs and try to sleep. Doctor's orders."

Phoebe didn't feel like fighting. She climbed to the third-floor bedroom and dropped onto her cot fully clothed. She was drifting off when the bedroom door banged open and Louisa rushed to her bedside.

Phoebe struggled up. "What is it, Louisa? Is it George?"

"No no," she said, kneeling beside her cot. "Sorry to scare you, but Dr. Bertram and I think we know how you both contracted typhus." She lifted the edge of the blanket. "Let me see your hand."

"What?"

"Your hand, the one you cut."

Puzzled, Phoebe held out her palm. "It's healing," she said. "It hurts, but when you have to use it all the time—"

"It hurts because it's infected. We thought so." Louisa tucked her arm back under the blanket. "Dr. Bertram examined George's wounds—they're infected too—and gave him some morphine. He thinks those bandages were infected when the nurse put them on."

"Infected? How?"

"If the bandages came off a soldier infected with typhus and weren't cleaned properly, you both introduced typhus into open wounds. You didn't have a chance."

"But the washerwomen are so careful about soiled bandages. They boil them, don't they?"

"Yes, but I got suspicious when Dr. Bertram said the hospital had stopped using the type of bandage you have last year."

"I'm confused," Phoebe said, rubbing her eyes. "What do you mean?"

"I think someone from outside—not one of *our* orderlies— gave infected bandages to Nurse Williams specifically for George. He was infected on purpose."

Phoebe groaned. "I've been afraid that someone might still try to kill George."

"The only accident was *you* contracting typhus too when you cut your hand and used the leftover bandage."

Phoebe closed her eyes to keep the room from spinning. "Which orderly gave her the bandages?"

"Dr. Bertram asked her." Louisa paused. "Nurse Williams said she hadn't seen him since the first day she worked here."

Phoebe curled into a ball on her side, and exhaustion washed over her. Was that orderly in league with the ambulance driver who'd shot her husband? Someone wasn't taking any chances. They wanted her husband dead, and they weren't going to wait for a court martial where he could testify to what he'd seen the driver steal.

The next morning, Louisa was already gone when Phoebe woke up. Her roommate's words washed over Phoebe. She had to protect George. He was in danger from the driver, but also from well-intentioned people like Nurse Williams, who Phoebe believed had only meant to help.

Last night, Louisa had stressed that more than half the typhus patients pulled through. Phoebe had tried to seem encouraged, but that meant that many, many of them died too. And George was already so very weak from his wounds and his mental anguish over the false charges.

And then there was Annie. Why hadn't she received an update about her daughter's condition?

An awful suspicion hit her then. Had a letter been delivered from Jane that Louisa was keeping from her until she was stronger? She must find out.

It took Phoebe fifteen minutes to get herself presentable enough to go downstairs. Clinging to the banister to walk upright and not attract attention, she made her way down to the surgical floor, took a few shaky breaths, and started down to the ground floor. She was halfway down when she had to sit. She pressed herself against the railing to keep out of the way. As Phoebe rested her head against the cold banister, she fought the cough rising in her throat.

Behind her, two attendants descending the staircase were discussing the healthiest men in the hospital. Phoebe's hearing sharpened. Drivers would arrive later that week to move a dozen healing men to convalescent homes outside the city. The attendants stepped around Phoebe, but one stopped and turned back. She forced a smile and waved him on his way.

Phoebe had to be well enough to be on hand when the drivers showed up. If the one she suspected came, she'd maneuver to walk him past George's open door. She'd drag George's bed around so if he were awake and alert, he could see into the hallway and then identify him when the time came.

She stood and swayed, grabbing the banister before she tumbled down the stairs. Her head felt like a cannonball, and the stairs undulated in a most disagreeable manner. She couldn't pass out in the lobby. She would go back upstairs and rest awhile, then come down later to move George's bed. The drivers weren't coming till later in the week.

Dragging her weary body back upstairs, Phoebe returned to their room, trusting that Louisa would check on George and report any changes she found. The rest of the day was a blur of restless sleeping, sitting by the fire shivering, and dragging herself downstairs for a meal. She wouldn't let someone come up two flights while it was possible for her to go down. She took food to George, who thrashed in a fitful sleep. She hated to wake him, but if nightmares tormented him as they did her own rest, sleep was a mixed blessing. Wiping a cool cloth over his face soothed him. He smiled at her gratefully and drifted off again.

Phoebe balanced her food tray on her lap, staring at it with distaste. The meal was the same as always: a bit of pork and army bread composed of sawdust and saleratus, which barely leavened the dough. The reconstituted dried blackberries looked to her fevered mind like a bowl of preserved cockroaches. The tea was no more than three dried huckleberry leaves to a quart of water. She had never in her life felt less like eating, but she knew she had to fight her infection and preserve what meager strength she had.

After she'd forced down a few bites, she set aside the food tray and stood. Phoebe grasped the head of George's cot and pulled with all her might, digging in her feet until the cot began to slide across the floor. George opened his eyes briefly, and she described her plan. "I'll try," he whispered. She stopped for a moment, so dizzy that she thought she would fall on her husband, then leaned down to pull again. She finally got the cot into a position where, when the door was open to the hallway, George could see anyone she brought by.

Bending to retrieve the food tray, Phoebe felt the room swirl violently. She hit the floor and everything went dark.

16

St. Albans, Vermont
Present Day

Still weak from being locked in the camper, Sofia pushed herself to sprint to the craft area where Amanda did her quilting demonstration. Avoiding the main lane, she ran instead behind the trees that shaded the meadow.

When she rounded a curve, she saw that Amanda's quilting frame was gone. Her friends must have already dismantled and loaded it into the back of her maroon van. Was Matthew in there too? Amanda was unpinning her last quilt from the clothesline while she chatted with two spectators.

Sofia slipped behind a tree near the van and pressed her back against the rough bark.

"Oh no," she heard Amanda say. "Jane Stickle did more than the quilt she's so famous for. She made smaller ones that she donated to the Ladies Hospital Aid Society. These were given to wounded soldiers. Some soldiers didn't even have blankets."

Sofia stiffened her shaking legs, prayed that Amanda wouldn't look her way, and sneaked to the back of her van. *Please don't let it be locked.* Holding her breath, she reached for the handle on the rear door.

The handle turned. Sofia crawled inside and pulled it partly closed. In the dim light, she searched frantically under the quilts and blankets piled inside. Matthew wasn't there. She wanted to cry. Where was he? He'd been gone more than six hours already.

She was crawling back to the door when her hand closed over something small. She gasped. *A wooden soldier painted blue!*

Matthew must have been there! But where was he now?

Had Amanda slipped away earlier and taken Matthew somewhere? Her home, maybe? She could have posted a Back Later sign like the others. Like Amanda, the other crafters were kept busy answering spectator questions and selling their goods. If Matthew had been lured into the van, no one would have noticed.

Sofia had no choice. Amanda was leaving, so she'd stow away in the back of her van and go home with her. If she'd taken Matthew for whatever misguided or confused reasons, Sofia had to reach him soon. Amanda was fragile and out of touch with reality, and Sofia would do everything she could not to hurt her—but she was going to get her son back.

She hid behind some boxes and pulled a blanket over her just before the van door opened again. She assumed that the muffled *plop* she heard was Amanda adding the last folded quilt. The back door of the van banged shut.

Soon another door slammed, and the engine roared to life. The van lurched ahead over the bumpy meadow. Sofia fell sideways, hitting her backbone on the side of the van.

Stifling her groan, she rubbed her back as they made it to the smoother lane. The van's speed picked up as they moved to the city streets; at least, Sofia assumed that's where they were. Outside the park, they chugged and swayed up one street and down the next. Huddled in the dark, it was impossible to tell how far they'd driven, but she tried to note other things. At one point, it felt as if they drove on a brick or cobblestone street. But she didn't smell anything distinctive like a bakery, or hear specific sounds like church bells to help pinpoint her route. Sofia tried to keep track of each turn Amanda made, but she finally gave up in confusion.

So instead, she saved her strength to act when the time was right. And the time would surely come. She gripped Matthew's wooden soldier as if it were a good luck charm.

It all added up, and Sofia felt blind for not seeing it before. The pieces fit together: Amanda's loneliness, her confusion at times between what was real and what was in her past, how often she mentioned Matthew's startling resemblance to her grandson, Joey.

After she'd jounced roughly from side to side for at least twenty minutes, the van braked, navigated one last, slow turn, and then stopped. The engine died.

Sofia held her breath. Would Amanda find her now? She could hear her singing, "I was seeing Nellie ho-o-ome, I was seeing Nellie home. And 'twas from Aunt Dinah's quilting party. I was seeing Nellie home." Then her door slammed. Instead of coming to the back of the van, her footsteps grew softer and softer.

After a full minute had passed, Sofia crawled to the rear of the van. In slow motion, she opened the left door an inch, waited, then swung it wide. Across the street were two stately older homes with a sad, rundown air about them, partially hidden by trees a century old. She waited, but not a car or pedestrian passed on the street.

Sofia slipped out of the van and peered cautiously around the corner. She was standing in the driveway of a formerly elegant three-story brick home. Its green shutters were peeling, and the cracked bricks in the sidewalk stuck up in places.

It's now or never, she thought, marching up to the front door. She lifted the iron knocker—a metal ring in a lion's mouth—and let it drop. A calico cat at the corner of the house meowed, then disappeared into the overgrown bushes.

She waited, then knocked again. A moment later, the ornately carved door swung open on creaky hinges.

"It's you!" Amanda blinked in confusion, then smiled broadly. "What a nice surprise. Come in."

Sofia stepped into the musty-smelling hallway, letting her eyes adjust to the dim interior. She decided to play her hunch. "I've come to say goodbye. Before I head home, I wanted to meet your grandson. I heard that he's visiting."

Amanda's face lit up. "Joey would love some company, but he's napping now."

"Could I wait?"

"Why, certainly. We'll have some iced tea in the parlor first."

"Thank you." Sofia felt a twinge of guilt for deliberately playing on the elderly lady's delusions in order to trick her, but she had to find Matthew. She followed Amanda down the dingy hall, past a flight of steep stairs, and into the parlor. Its threadbare needlepoint rug spoke of magnificence from a bygone era. A small marble fireplace filled one end of the narrow parlor, and yellowing photographs in ornate frames paraded across the mantel.

"You wait here," Amanda told her, "while I get the tea."

As soon as the older woman disappeared, Sofia quickly searched the room for a phone but couldn't find one.

She moved to the mantel for a closer look at the photographs. The one that caught Sofia's eye was a family photo. In it were four people—an older couple, a young man, and a small boy. Sofia's heart constricted. The boy could have been Matthew, the similarities were so striking. It was too bad Amanda's son and grandson had relocated to Alaska.

On the coffee table was a huge family Bible. Sofia lifted the thick heavy cover and looked inside. The information so meticulously chronicled for several generations took her breath away.

On the page listing births and deaths was a small photo of Joey alongside the dates of his birth—and death. He'd died at the age of ten, the same age as Matthew.

Washington, D.C.
December 1862

"Phoebe. Phoebe!"

Strong, capable hands lifted her to a sitting position and leaned her against the wall.

"Phoebe, it's me, Louisa. You fainted." The nurse rubbed Phoebe's wrists and felt her forehead. "You're burning up. Come on."

She supported her all the way to their third-floor bedroom, where she tucked her in. "Now stay here," Louisa said. "I mean it. Consider yourself quarantined until Dr. Bertram gives you leave to come downstairs."

"But I can't—"

"I'll check on George and feed him," Louisa interrupted. "I promise. You must take care of yourself. You're dreadfully ill." She gave her another sip of water. "I must get back to my ward now."

Phoebe closed her eyes wearily. She trusted Louisa to check on George when her hectic schedule allowed, but she couldn't sit in there and protect him and watch him. Thanks to Phoebe, he could now see all those passing his open door, but he wouldn't be able to defend himself if that driver spotted him.

Phoebe had unintentionally made it more dangerous for George, and now she was two floors away from him, in quarantine. Then, with a silent prayer, she lost consciousness.

She drifted in and out of awareness for two days. Awake or asleep, her thoughts were a frightening jumble of worry about her husband and herself and what would happen to their children if they both died from typhus.

More than once, Phoebe awoke from nightmares to find Louisa sponging her face and limbs with cool water. Phoebe felt guilty for using Louisa's meager rest times and for filling their room with illness. Twice Louisa brought her tea and toast, but Phoebe couldn't swallow the toast. She drank the tea, but it tasted worse than usual.

"George?" Phoebe asked the second time.

"Doing well, slightly better than you," Louisa said. "He knows you're sick and must stay in bed."

"Letters?" Phoebe asked.

"What letters?" Louisa refilled her cup with tea. "From home, you mean? No, there haven't been any." Her eyes were warm with sympathy. "You'll receive news soon. With hundreds of troops moving this week, the trains are full. That always delays mail."

Phoebe hoped that was true. The nights were especially long. With Louisa on night shift now, Phoebe was alone. She slept fitfully, desperate for rest, but fearing the nightmares that plagued her. Phoebe awoke during the second night and was surprised to see the young Italian medical student sitting by her fire, whittling shavings to add to the basket of chopped wood. Then he built up her fire and left without a sound.

It was morning the next time she opened her eyes, and Louisa was washing up in preparation for her own sleep. Phoebe told her about finding Marco de Luca tending their fire during the night.

Louisa nodded. "When I came here, I expected to be treated like a lowly servant. Except for Dr. Kauffmann, who is gruff with the other surgeons as well as nurses, I was pleased to find myself treated with the utmost courtesy by most doctors." She grinned. "It's my private opinion, though, that nurses do the hardest work of anyone in the army." She crawled into her own cot. "Except maybe the mules."

Phoebe coughed hard into her pillow and struggled to catch her breath. "Is there any word on when the soldiers will be moved to the convalescent homes?" She still planned to be downstairs when the drivers came through.

Louisa pulled her blanket up to her chin and rolled on her side to face Phoebe. "They showed up just before the end of my shift tonight."

"Tonight?" Phoebe cried.

"Yes, they surprised us all. Half a dozen drivers were in and out, but in the chaos of preparing patients to leave, I don't know if they got near the medicine cupboard or not."

"But George!" She struggled to get out of bed. "He was left unprotected!"

Louisa was out of bed in a flash, gently pushing Phoebe back down on her cot. "Shhhh. George is just fine."

"But I have to go to him. If the driver who shot him saw him—"

"He didn't," Louisa said firmly. "I guessed your reason for rearranging his room to be near the door. I moved him back out of sight. And when the ambulances arrived, I borrowed a key from the ward master. I covered George with an extra quilt and locked his door. He was safe. I opened it back up after they left to let some heat in." She patted Phoebe's hand.

Phoebe squeezed her friend's hand. If she and George made it through, it would be in large part because of this warmhearted nurse. One day, she hoped to find a way to repay her.

The following day was again a blur for Phoebe. Hours blended together, and the gloomy overcast days made it nearly impossible to tell whether it was morning or afternoon. When total darkness fell, she began another long night's fight with weariness and pain. At night, people swam in her vision, looking odd and yet familiar. Was she awake or asleep? She couldn't tell. Voices echoed oddly, as if they were speaking to her underwater.

The next morning when Phoebe opened her eyes, it immediately struck her. The headache was much better. Gingerly she moved her head from side to side. It wasn't gone, but it had diminished. And she'd stopped shaking with the chills.

Louisa arrived after her night shift and smiled in delight. "Better this morning?" she asked. She set down a tray of tea and toast. "Maybe you'll feel like eating."

Phoebe twisted around to sit up in bed. "I'll try. I need to get my strength back."

Louisa wrapped a shawl around Phoebe's shoulders, then pulled a chair close while she sipped her tea. "This tastes good. It has sugar in it," Phoebe said.

"Honey," Louisa corrected, "but don't tell. Cook would have my head."

Phoebe had nearly finished her tea when someone knocked on the door. "Yes?" Louisa called.

Marco de Luca opened the door and waved a letter. "Guess who has letter from Vermont?"

"News of Annie!" Phoebe reached eagerly for it. While she opened it, Marco scraped ashes from the fireplace into a tin box and laid their fire.

Phoebe skimmed Jane's letter and then fell back against the iron headboard. "She's better." Tears welled up and then coursed down her cheeks. "Our Annie has pulled through." She laughed as she cried, wiping tears on her sleeve.

"I carry *buone* news to husband," Marco said from where he coaxed the kindling into flame. "It cheers him up, no?"

"Yes, it will cheer him up, but I'll tell him." Phoebe swung her legs out of bed.

Louisa shook her head. "No, you will rest at least one more day. You're much too weak to be on the stairs."

Swaying as her head spun, Phoebe swallowed her frustration

and nodded. "Then please do tell Mr. Ashford, Dr. de Luca."

Louisa refilled Phoebe's cup. "Your husband's fever actually broke yesterday, while you were still delirious. Dr. de Luca can also tell him you're much better today." She turned to the young medical student. "If Mrs. Ashford stays in bed today, I'll help her downstairs this evening to have supper with her husband."

"Si, I tell him. Right away." He tipped an invisible hat in Phoebe's direction and left.

"I'll take the tray back to the kitchen and write my reports, then come back to sleep." Louisa felt Phoebe's dampish sheets. "You need clean sheets now that your fever has broken. And let me loan you a clean nightgown. You've sweated through yours."

Phoebe knew she ought to protest. The men in the ward deserved Louisa's attention more than she did. But resting today in clean sheets—especially now that she'd heard good news about both George and Annie—sounded like heaven.

It was only ten minutes later when a laundress came to change her sheet. The woman grabbed Phoebe's blanket off the bed. "Wrap up in this and sit by the fire." Then the cheerful laundress gave a sharp tug, pulling the rough cotton sheet off her bed.

Phoebe froze.

When the tucked-in sheet was yanked loose, something else slid out from under her mattress—her stolen pages from the medicine log.

Lord, please don't let her notice! Phoebe begged.

Phoebe jumped up, ignoring her dizziness. "I can finish," she said. "Just leave me the clean sheet."

"Nurse Alcott would tan my hide." With a snap, the grinning woman shook the clean sheet out over the bed. "I have strict instructions."

"Then let me help. I know how busy you are." Phoebe moved to where the pages stuck out beneath the mattress. She bent quickly to tuck in the sheet, pushing the notebook pages back under the mattress as she did.

The laundress left a few moments later, and Phoebe crawled back into her newly changed bed. Had the laundress seen the papers? Would she know what they were?

Would she tell anyone what she'd seen?

17

St. Albans, Vermont
Present Day

Sofia stared at the dates. Amanda's grandson hadn't moved away. He'd *died*.

She had to tell Officer Quimby. At shuffling sounds behind her, Sofia quickly closed the Bible and sat in a chair. Amanda carried in two glasses of iced tea on a silver tray, plus a dish of lemon slices. Her hands shook visibly as she set the tray on a small marble-topped table.

"Here we go," Amanda said. "The perfect way to end the day."

Sofia gulped the cold tea. "This hits the spot."

Although the dim room had first given the illusion of coolness, it now felt oppressive. And it wasn't just the unseasonable warmth.

Just then, from overhead, came a muffled thud.

Heart pounding, Sofia tried to sound casual. "Is that Joey moving around upstairs? Maybe he's awake now."

Amanda's hands fluttered over her lap like fragile butterflies. "Oh no, not yet. That's just Callie Mae, my calico cat." Amanda clucked her tongue. "Such a naughty kitty."

Sofia had seen the cat outside when she'd arrived. And since Joey had been dead for five years according to the record in the Bible, that noise upstairs had to be Matthew.

Straining to keep her face and voice neutral, Sofia asked, "Do you think I could have some more tea?" She held out her empty glass. "With sugar?"

"Of course." Amanda sprang up and took her glass. "I'll be right back."

After she left, Sofia kicked off her shoes, then raced on silent stocking feet back down the hall and up the wide staircase. At the top of the stairs was a landing with hallways stretching both right and left, as well as straight ahead.

Which hallway was above the parlor where she'd heard the sound? She didn't have time to make a mistake.

She slipped to the first door on her right. It was locked. She knocked lightly and pressed her ear to the door. No response.

At the door across the hall, she repeated the tapping and listening. Still nothing.

Her nerves stretched to the breaking point as she listened for Amanda.

The frayed carpet runner muffled her steps as she raced to the third door, then the fourth. No sound, and all locked. Where was her son? Behind the fifth locked door, however, she heard someone moving around inside.

"Matthew?" she murmured through the keyhole. "It's Mom."

When there was no response, she threw caution to the winds and rattled the knob. She had to get to her son. She slammed her shoulder against the door, but it held fast. She stifled a sob of pain and frustration. He could be hurt—or dying. Who knew what Amanda had done to him in her confusion?

Bending over to peer through the keyhole, Sofia found a skeleton key hanging on a metal cup hook beside the door. *Finally*, she thought, *a break*. After several tries, the rusty key unlocked the door, and Sofia swung it wide. Moth-eaten material at a cracked window swayed in the stale air stirred by opening the door. The smells of mildew and mothballs almost turned her stomach.

Just then, there was a piercing scream from behind her. "Joey! No!"

Before Sofia could turn around, a sharp blow grazed her left shoulder. Her knees buckled, and she was pushed hard from behind. She fell into the dim room. The door was immediately slammed—and locked—behind her.

Washington, D.C.
December 1862

After sleeping all day, Phoebe awoke feeling that the worst was behind her. She chided herself for worrying that the laundress had seen her notebook pages. After supper with George, she would ask Louisa to go through them with her. Louisa would understand the writing and notice discrepancies that would slide past Phoebe.

However, by the time she'd eaten with George and they'd rejoiced over Annie's recovery, she felt as if she'd run ten miles. After climbing back up to the third floor, she was happy to collapse into bed. She'd wait until the next day to go over the medical log pages.

It was pitch-black when Phoebe was aroused by a soft noise. She was shivering uncontrollably. *Not the fever again!*

Then she realized the fire was close to going out, and she was shaking simply because the room had grown so very cold. But what was that slithering sound? Had their rat traps failed?

She peered through the dimness, stared hard, and made out a dark form standing inside the door. Louisa must be checking on her. Phoebe started to speak, but her greeting died in her throat. When the shadow moved into the room between her and the fireplace, it was clear that the person wore trousers—a man.

Heart thudding against her ribs, Phoebe lay still and tried to make out the shadow's identity. While she was at death's door, she knew some of the staff had come and quietly rebuilt the fire during the night.

But who was this, sliding along the side of the room, searching in her belongings—even flipping through her Bible?

He moved past the fireplace without stoking the fire, and at that moment, Phoebe was terrified. The intruder wasn't there to help her, so what was he doing in her room? She considered screaming, but would anyone hear her, tucked away on the third floor? Would the intruder silence her before she could rouse anyone to help her? As the shadow turned in her direction, Phoebe shut her eyes and forced herself to breathe in a shallow, slow cadence, as if still asleep. There were more soft footsteps. She hoped he was leaving.

Without warning, she was jostled as something—*an arm?*—was thrust under her mattress once, then twice. He was looking for the pages from the medical log book! She moaned and twisted, as if having a nightmare.

The arm was quickly withdrawn. Running footsteps crossed the dark room. The door opened and closed quietly, leaving Phoebe trembling with both terror and cold. She slipped out of bed and pushed her own arm under the mattress. She slid her arm back and forth several times, then sat back on her heels. A sob escaped her.

The pages of notes—the only evidence she had to prove her husband's innocence—were gone.

Phoebe added a log to their fire, then dressed in the frigid room. She'd never get back to sleep now. She had to tell Louisa that they'd had a prowler in their room.

Before she'd finished dressing, Louisa popped in to see if she wanted breakfast before the larder was emptied.

"Close the door," Phoebe whispered. She told Louisa about their visitor and fought back tears over what she'd lost.

Louisa pulled her chair near the fire and sat. "But how would an orderly or steward even know *you* had the pages, assuming someone noticed they were torn out?"

"At first I thought the laundress must have told someone." Phoebe bit her lip. "But there was someone nearby when I tore out the pages. I hoped at the time that he hadn't seen me. At least, he never said anything."

"Who was it?"

Phoebe sighed. "That Italian medical student."

Louisa was silent for a moment, staring into the fire. "Should I see if anyone can vouch for his whereabouts during the night?"

"He wasn't in here more than five minutes. No one could know where someone was the entire night." Phoebe twisted her hands, then made up her mind. "I'll talk to him."

However, when she went in search of the medical student, he was gone. According to the ward master, a driver had arrived before breakfast to transport several wounded officers to the Officers' Hospital. Marco de Luca had gone along to help.

Phoebe waited at the front door of the hospital, but the limping driver returned alone. "Did the young Italian doctor stay with the officers?" she asked him.

"No. Said he felt like walking back."

Phoebe waited in the lobby, alternately sitting and pacing, but three hours later the student doctor hadn't arrived. Phoebe didn't know where he'd gone, but over the morning she'd convinced herself that he had indeed taken her evidence of morphine theft to show someone, perhaps someone in charge of the whole drug-smuggling scheme.

And if those thugs knew their plan was no longer a secret, she and George both were in mortal danger.

Near noon, Dr. Dickerson came downstairs, white coat tails flying, and called to her. "Have you seen Dr. de Luca?" he demanded, exasperated. "He is to assist me in surgery." His glance focused on Phoebe as if suddenly realizing who she was. "Mrs. Ashford? I examined your husband this morning."

"Yes?"

"He has mended sufficiently to be moved."

Phoebe's heart leaped. "Moved where?" She swallowed hard around the sudden lump in her throat. "To a convalescent home?" she asked, hoping against hope.

"Of course not." The surgeon stared past her and out the window. "He'll go to prison to await trial."

That afternoon, Phoebe couldn't bring herself to discuss Dr. Dickerson's report with George. But after spending several hours with him, reading to him and talking about the children, Phoebe had to admit Louisa was right: She wasn't totally well yet, and George deserved the truth.

In tears she apologized to George for failing him, but George laid a finger over her lips. "No, darling." Awkwardly he wrapped his good arm around her shoulders. "You have done everything possible—and taken too many risks, I suspect—to prove my innocence. It's in God's hands now."

She headed back to bed then, unable to get Dr. Dickerson's dire words out of her mind. After a long nap, Phoebe paced back and forth across the tiny bedroom. There had to be something else she could do. Had the student doctor returned yet? She'd believed that he was her friend, but if he'd stolen those papers and reported her to someone involved in the drug ring, she had badly misjudged him.

Settle down, she scolded herself. *Do something useful while you think.*

She'd begged Louisa for something productive to do during her recuperation, and her roommate had brought up a basket containing cleaned uniforms that needed mending. "You're forbidden to meddle with fleshy arms and legs, but console yourself with mending cotton and woolen ones." Phoebe nodded. She'd sew. She knew from experience that when her fingers were busy, her mind often worked better too.

Phoebe dragged her chair over to the window where the light was better, grabbed the uniform on the top of the pile, and threaded her needle. Her agitated heart quieted as the needle slipped in and out, in and out, slowly repairing the garment. As she brought wholeness to a torn piece of cloth, the Lord smoothed her own ragged edges and brought wholeness to her thinking.

After half an hour, Phoebe stood to stretch her aching back. She still had a mild headache, and her joints ached as if she were older than her own mother. She stood by the window and absentmindedly watched a long train of army wagons trundle by below. The perpetual rumble lasted from morning till night, so constant that she rarely noticed it anymore. Ambulances rattled by with busy surgeons, wagons took nurses for an airing, and groups of convalescents went to be fitted for artificial limbs. Barouches with invalid officers rolled by sometimes. Once she'd even seen a carriage from the wealthier district loaded with pretty children, black coachmen, footmen, and maids.

Phoebe watched as a cart rumbled into view below. It carried several rough coffins, but no mourners followed. She grieved for the dead and their families.

Gallant riders followed on horseback, some in scarlet-lined riding cloaks and sashes, all wearing high boots and bright spurs. Louisa had once remarked that "their beards and mustaches made plain faces handsome and handsome faces heroic."

Phoebe laughed aloud, remembering something else Louisa had said. Once, when resting outside on the porch, she had commented on the women going by. "They wear three-story bonnets with overhanging balconies of flowers. All I can say is that they are dressed in the worst possible taste." She'd studied them moving away down the street. "And they walk like ducks."

One wagon, half filled with soldiers, now pulled up directly under her at the front of the hotel hospital. Phoebe pressed her face close to the glass and looked straight down. Two men rode on the seat, and Phoebe squinted for a better look. One of them was Marco de Luca. He jumped down, said something to the driver, and disappeared into the hospital.

When the ambulance driver glanced around and up, she recognized the cheerful young man who'd flirted with the young nurses the day he'd taken some soldiers back to their regiments. Why was he just sitting there now?

Just then, Marco rushed out, spoke to the driver, and handed him a small package. Phoebe pressed even closer to the glass. They talked for a moment, and the driver nodded. He removed his cap, scratched a surprising bald spot on top, and replaced his cap. *Too bad he's losing his hair so young,* Phoebe thought.

Something nagged at her. She frowned. What was it? Then it hit her. George's description of the driver who'd shot him: big arms, rattlesnake tattoo, young but looked older because he was already going bald.

Was *he* the driver who'd shot her husband, instead of the rude driver she disliked so much? Had the medical student given him her log book pages? And what had the young Italian just now run out to give the driver? Drugs? Were those two good-natured men phonies, putting on an act while actually part of the drug scheme she wanted to expose?

Her heart beat so hard she had to sit down.

Was that "nice" young driver the man who'd tried to kill her husband?

18

St. Albans, Vermont
Present Day

Stunned by the vicious attack, Sofia whirled around and pounded on the door. "Let me out, Amanda!"

There was no answer. Sofia turned and leaned her back against the door, her shoulder throbbing. After a moment, her eyes adjusted to the dim room. Yellowed window shades had been pulled against the afternoon sun. From beside a massive wooden wardrobe stepped an elderly man in uniform.

Sofia gasped. "Who are you?" She frantically searched the room without waiting for his answer. "Matthew?"

Then she saw him in a corner of the darkened room, tucked into a bed with heavy oak posts. In a flash, Sofia was by his side. She grasped his hand in one of hers and pushed the damp hair off his forehead with the other. Despite the stuffiness of the room, he didn't feel feverish. She shook him gently, but he didn't respond. Did he have a head injury? Or had he been given something to make him sleep?

She couldn't see him clearly, so she raised the roller shade, which stirred a small cloud of dust. She felt the rise and fall of Matthew's chest; he was breathing steadily.

She pounded on the door again. "Amanda, let us out!" she called. "Please! My son needs a doctor!"

There was no answer. Was Amanda even out there?

Then someone in the darkness touched her arm, and she jumped. Up close, the older man's skin was a sickly gray. "Your son will sleep it off, I think," he said.

Sofia recognized the long beard. "You're the man who got dizzy by Amanda's quilt frame."

He nodded. "There must have been some drug in the lemonade she offered me. I was fine before then." He pointed to his round glasses. "And she switched my specs too," he said, a wry tone in his voice. "She took mine off to wipe my face, then handed me a different pair. I expect these belonged to her husband. His stronger prescription disoriented me at first."

"I don't understand," Sofia said, rubbing her sore shoulder. "Why capture you too? You don't really resemble her husband."

"No, but I portray a surgeon in the reenactments, like her husband did." He rubbed his hands on his blue trousers. "I assume that she gave your son lemonade laced with some drug, but she gave him too much for his size. She panicked when he didn't come around when she expected, so she wanted a doctor to examine him."

Sofia frowned. "But you're not a real doctor."

"You and I understand that, but Mrs. Witte is a bit confused."

"How did she get you to come here with her?" Sofia couldn't imagine the small woman manhandling this soldier into her van.

The older gentleman looked sheepish. "She said her ancestor had been an army surgeon in the Civil War, and she had some of his instruments that she was willing to sell. I came to look at them. I didn't know about your son until she led me upstairs to see the instruments. When I walked in here, she locked the door behind me and yelled at me to take care of him. She refused to believe that I'm not really a doctor."

Sofia went back to sit by the bed. Amanda wasn't as frail as she looked if she'd managed to drag or carry a ten-year-old boy upstairs, even one small for his age as Matthew was.

How much of the sleeping drug had the demented woman given him? She wished their fellow captive truly was a doctor. Matthew was breathing steadily, but when was he going to wake up?

In fact, *would* he wake up?

Washington, D.C.
January 1863

The ambulance driver flapped his reins and pulled away from the hospital. Mind racing, Phoebe paced around the bedroom for ten minutes, trying to decide what to do.

Everything in her wanted to run downstairs, corner the medical student, and demand some answers. Questions whirled in her head, one after the other. Was Marco the intruder who'd searched her room and stolen the pages from the medicine log? Where had he been all morning? What was in the package he'd just handed to the driver? Was the student in league with the man who'd shot George?

Perhaps all of this added up to nothing outside her overactive imagination.

Phoebe was desperate for answers, but she knew she had to be shrewd when she confronted him. She couldn't let him see her suspicions.

For one thing, Marco de Luca could be completely innocent. Or, in contrast, he could be part of a large drug operation. And then her heart dropped. Marco worked closely with his mentor, Dr. Bertram, the man she'd seen twice in the back garden, giving mysterious packages to a cloaked woman. *The two men must be in it together.*

When a nurse brought her a bowl of soup for lunch, Phoebe gave her a message for the young medical student. "Please have him come see me as soon as he has a break." The nurse raised an eyebrow, but she agreed to pass along the message.

Phoebe was mending a shirt by the fire when someone knocked. "Come in," she called.

Marco stood in the doorway. "You want to see me, no?"

Phoebe gave him a disarming smile. "I was sewing by the window earlier when you returned with a driver I want to talk to. You came inside and then returned with a package for him."

"You see that up here?"

She forced a laugh, hoping it sounded lighthearted. "The days get long, and there is much to entertain oneself watching the parade below the window."

"Si. True." He joined her at the fire. "The morning mail is gone, but a dying soldier whittles *giocattoli*—er, toys—to mail home. The wife expects first baby, the child he never sees. But toys make him part of child's life, no? He wants toys to go before he dies. Driver agrees to take toys to train station, which sends mail tonight." He shrugged. "It is small thing to do."

Phoebe shook her head. "No, not a small thing at all." She glanced at him out of the corner of her eye. Was he telling her the truth? Keeping her head down and her eyes on her sewing, she asked, "Do you know the driver's name?"

"Why?"

"I wanted to thank him for a courtesy he did my husband."

"Sorry. I do not know the name." He stood to leave. "I must go for surgery, or Dr. Bertram will have my hide, as they say, no?" He laughed and brushed a hand over his hair, then left, closing the door behind him. Within a minute the door flew back open. "I remember," he said hurriedly. "Other drivers call him Rhett."

"Rhett? Thank you."

"*Prego.*" He smiled. "And Happy New Year."

Phoebe blinked in surprise. She'd forgotten that today was January 1, 1863.

That evening, Phoebe related her conversation with Marco to Louisa. Her roommate frowned. "I'm not saying his story about mailing toys to the young wife isn't true, but I don't know who he's talking about. None of the surgical nurses mentioned such a case." She shrugged. "That doesn't necessarily mean anything. We don't have time to discuss every case."

Then Louisa reached out and gripped Phoebe's hand. The look on her face made Phoebe's blood run cold. "What is it?" Phoebe asked.

"The ward master gave me a list of soldiers to get ready for tomorrow's pickups."

Phoebe's breath caught in her throat. "George?"

Louisa nodded slowly. "Your husband is scheduled for the last pickup of the day."

"To go . . ." She couldn't finish.

The silence hung on until Louisa broke it grimly. "To go to prison."

In a split second, a scene flashed before Phoebe's eyes: The cheery young ambulance driver was taking George away to deliver him to prison. But George never arrived.

Not alive, anyway.

That night, after tossing and turning for hours, Phoebe gave up trying to sleep. She had to prevent George from being taken to prison tomorrow. But how?

After midnight, she was no closer to sleep. Pulling her coat on over her dressing gown, she slipped downstairs. Maybe a cup of weak tea, or even plain hot water, would relax her.

Suddenly she had an overwhelming need to see George, despite the late hour. She just wanted to hug him, kiss him, and hold him, and be held herself. But when she slipped into his room, she heard his heavy breathing and knew he was sleeping deeply. She sighed. He probably hadn't been told yet. Since it might be his last good night's sleep for a long time, she backed out, relocked the door, and headed to the kitchen.

She poured a cup of hot water through a strainer of old tea leaves for a bit of flavor and then sat at the rugged oak table. She had to save George. After he was picked up, she'd have no more chances.

Despite the hot tea, Phoebe grew colder in the drafty room. Eventually she noticed that the back door hadn't latched properly. She moved to close it, but her eye caught a wavering light outside. She froze. It was a lamp at the back fence. She wouldn't let that woman get away again.

Phoebe regretted that she hadn't worn shoes downstairs. Her stockings would have to do this time. Wrapping her coat tightly around her, she slipped outside and around the corner of the building, her eyes on the doctor and the nurse at the fence. It was ten long minutes before the doctor turned and, lamp held before him, headed back to the kitchen. Phoebe caught his expression in the lamplight. He looked happy, as if he'd been with someone he loved.

The woman moved away, but Phoebe had to wait until the doctor was inside before racing across the dark yard. When she let herself out through the wrought-iron gate, she didn't see the woman, but Phoebe knew the direction she'd gone. She wouldn't get away this time.

Reaching the corner, Phoebe spotted the woman walking swiftly only half a block ahead. Phoebe picked up her dragging nightgown, and with the frigid wind blowing at her legs, she ran down the street. Her stockinged feet barely made a sound.

She caught up to the woman and grabbed her arm hard. "Stop!" she yelled as she yanked her around.

The woman screamed and tried to pull away.

"Oh no you don't," Phoebe said through gritted teeth. "I want answers, and I want them now."

"Who are you?" the woman cried. "Let go of me!"

Gasping for breath, Phoebe kept her grip tight on the woman's cloak and peered into her face. "I've seen you take morphine from one of our surgeons three times now. Don't bother denying it. What would the other staff at my hospital think?"

"Let go of me!" the woman snapped. "I've done nothing wrong."

"Then why sneak around?"

"I'm not sneaking around. Our hospital performs more amputations than yours, and we often run low on morphine. Sometimes our surgeons need to borrow some to get us through until our supply is refilled."

"Then why collect it over the back fence at midnight?" Phoebe demanded. "An honest person would come in the front door during the day."

The woman's tone was frosty. "You're obviously not a nurse. What do you think I do from sunrise until long after dark? The requirements of the wounded never stop." Weariness crept into her voice. "Yes, I could sail in through the front doors late at night after everyone is bedded down and wake them all up. Would your night nurses thank me for that?"

That could be true, Phoebe realized, but she didn't believe her. A person could enter through the front doors quietly. "I saw the look on Doctor Bertram's face. He loves you, or thinks he does. He's old enough to be your father. But I suppose a few kisses and batting your eyes at him—"

The woman's eyes blazed at that. "You think I'm using my feminine wiles to acquire morphine?"

"If he thinks he's in love with you and that you return his feel-ings, he might be foolish enough to believe you want the morphine for amputations." Phoebe poked at the woman's drawstring reticule and heard glass bottles clink together. "You're selling it to the highest bidder when our own men need it."

The woman didn't respond, but she peered closely at Phoebe's face, then glanced down at her nightgown and stockinged feet. "You sound delirious, dear. Go back to the hospital while I return to work." She clutched her reticule close. "And if you don't believe what I told you, feel free to ask my sweet *father* why he gives me painkillers." She turned, and with cloak flying behind her, strode off down the street.

Her father? Phoebe watched the nurse for half a block. *Dr. Bertram was her father?* Was that possible? Shivering violently, she headed back to the Union Hotel Hospital. Had his look of pleasure simply been that of a man delighted to see his daughter? She felt like such a fool.

Of course, just because Dr. Bertram believed the drugs were for her hospital didn't mean they were. That could be only the story she'd told him. It could be for a private patient, someone who could pay an enormous price, like Mary Todd Lincoln.

Drugs were disappearing from their hospital, and Louisa agreed with her about that. George had seen the ambulance driver stealing morphine, and he'd nearly paid for the knowledge with his life more than once. One way or another, Phoebe knew she had barely ten hours to find the answers and save her husband.

She would do it, or die trying.

19

St. Albans, Vermont
Present Day

"Matthew?" Sofia bent over her son. "Please wake up. It's Mom. I'm here." The silence stretched on until Sofia thought she'd crack from the strain. Suddenly her head snapped up, and she met the soldier's eye.

He nodded. He'd heard it too—a floorboard creaking.

Amanda was in the hall, her footsteps creeping closer.

The actor placed a finger at his lips, came nearer to Sofia, and whispered, "Let's trick her into opening the door."

"How?"

"Go along with her delusion." He moved to the door and raised his voice. "Amanda?"

No answer.

"Amanda? It's Dr. Richards." He paused. Feet shuffled on the other side of the door, then stopped. "Joey wants his grandmother."

After a long pause, Amanda called, "Joey? Joey, are you all right?"

"No," the actor said. "He's not. He was conscious for a moment and asked for you, but he slipped back into unconsciousness again."

"What's wrong with him?" she asked, her thin voice quivering.

"I don't know, but we must go to the hospital," he said. "I need to run some tests, and I don't have the right equipment here."

Sofia tiptoed over to the door to yank it open the second Amanda unlocked it—if she did.

After an interminable length of time, a key was inserted into the lock and turned. Amanda opened the door, cried out when she saw Sofia, and raised a fireplace poker to attack.

You're not getting me again!

Sofia ducked away from the poker and came up behind Amanda. As the older woman turned to take another swing at her, Sofia grabbed the poker, wrenched it from Amanda's grasp, and threw it. It skittered across the hard wooden floor and hit the wall. Then she pinned Amanda's arms to her sides.

The wiry woman struggled. Then, breaking into sobs, Amanda suddenly crumpled in Sofia's arms.

After calling information on Amanda's kitchen phone, Sofia called the office at the reenactment and asked for Officer Quimby.

"Jake Clark had a solid alibi," he said when he got to the phone.

"That doesn't matter now," Sofia told him. She gave him Amanda's address and asked him to bring Sergeant Poole with him. Then she called Jim to give him the good news.

"Thank God," he said. "The kids and I will be right there."

Half an hour later, Officer Quimby stood by quietly while Sergeant Poole questioned Amanda. Eyes downcast, Amanda huddled in her chair, looking small and deflated. Sofia appreciated the gentle way the sergeant handled the old woman. Despite what she'd done, Sofia knew her dementia was to blame.

"It was pretty much the way your mom figured it," Sergeant Poole explained to Matthew. "It started when Mrs. Witte confused her deceased grandson with you. At her age, sometimes the mind plays tricks."

Sofia pulled her younger son close. He was awake now, but still groggy.

Amanda studied each of their faces, then cocked her head to one side. Tears quietly slid down her cheeks, meandering as they followed her wrinkles. "You're Sofia, aren't you?" she whispered. "Did I hit you?"

Sofia nodded and rubbed her shoulder.

Amanda's mouth twisted as she wiped her face on a lacy handkerchief. "I'm so sorry. Please forgive me. I just didn't want to spend another day here alone." Her hands shook as she folded and refolded the lilac-scented handkerchief. Then her face brightened. "But Joey is well, isn't he?" She turned to Matthew. "I've missed you so much."

Sergeant Poole patted Amanda lightly on the shoulder. "Mrs. Witte? Could you make me a cup of tea?"

"Tea?" Behind her tiny oval glasses, Amanda's watery eyes brightened. "Yes, of course, right away. It's such a treat to have company." She bustled off toward the kitchen.

When she was out of earshot, Sofia turned to Sergeant Poole. "What will happen to her?"

The sergeant shook his head. "She's pretty confused. She skips from past to present and back again so easily. When she loses touch with reality, she honestly thinks your son is her grandson and this gentleman is her deceased husband." He lowered his voice. "Her son is still alive, but we haven't been able to get in touch with him yet. Unless you folks press charges, she'll most likely end up in a nursing home. I've already called a doctor."

Sofia couldn't imagine Jim wanting to press charges. She certainly didn't want to. She could hear Amanda singing in the kitchen; it made her heart ache. "Should I go help her?"

"No, let her be," said Sergeant Poole. "I'll wait until the doctor comes. You're all free to go."

"Shouldn't we say goodbye?" Sofia asked.

"It would be hard for her to see you leave, with her thinking her grandson and husband are alive." He glanced toward the kitchen. "Let's not put her through that."

Sofia nodded, and they slipped quietly out of the house. She couldn't believe it had only been eight hours since Matthew went missing—the longest eight hours of her life. After hugging her children more tightly than usual, she let them go home with Jim. Officer Quimby would give her a lift back to the parking lot to drive the camper back to Cabot Falls.

As the officer backed them out of Amanda's driveway, Sofia felt an odd combination of joy and sorrow—joy at Matthew's safe return, but sorrow for the woman who would experience the loss of her loved ones all over again.

Washington, D.C.
January 1863

Grateful that the hospital was unlocked all night, Phoebe crept back into the kitchen, nearly frozen. Then she realized that the open-door policy meant that anyone could have stolen her log book pages, whether it had been someone on staff or someone from the outside world. With shaking hands she brewed a cup of tea and carried it upstairs. She managed only four hours of broken sleep, but she awoke with new resolve. She'd talk to George and reassure him that she'd never give up the fight, even after he was taken to prison. She'd prove his innocence somehow.

But can I do it before he is executed? She firmly pushed that thought away.

She was outside George's room when she heard a loud "Pssst!" behind her. Louisa was waving wildly at her. Had she heard new information about George? Phoebe raced back down the hall.

"I've been watching for you." Louisa glanced over her shoulder. "I have an idea for how you can catch the ambulance driver. Come back up to our room. I have something for you." Only then did Phoebe notice the burlap bag Louisa carried.

Burning with questions, Phoebe followed her upstairs to their room. There Louisa dumped a pile of clean clothing onto her cot. "For me?" Phoebe unfolded a clean, mended Yankee uniform.

Louisa closed their door. "I believe your husband saw the ambulance driver steal morphine."

Phoebe fought back tears. "You do?" She'd been worried that Louisa was simply humoring her.

"I admit that I wasn't sure at first," Louisa said. "Every soldier suspected of desertion says he's wrongfully accused." She sat down on the bed. "But once I started watching the medicine cupboard and checking the notebook, I found that it didn't add up."

"But this uniform? Is it for George to wear to prison?"

"No." Louisa held it up to Phoebe. "It's for a plan that might have a small chance of working."

Phoebe felt a flutter of hope. "A small chance is better than no chance."

Phoebe's eyes opened wide as Louisa spelled out her idea. Louisa wanted Phoebe to dress in the discarded uniform. "I'll dirty your face a bit and hide your hair under the cap pulled down low," she said. "We'll add some crutches, and you'll walk with your head down."

"Where will I go?"

"I've put you on the list for soldiers headed to convalescent homes. The wagon comes awhile before the one scheduled for your husband. I'll tell the driver you were dropped off here by mistake—you won't ever occupy a bed." Louisa eyed Phoebe critically. "Other women have disguised themselves as soldiers and spies, so I see no reason why you can't masquerade as one yourself."

"After I get on the wagon with the other men, then what?"

"That's for you to figure out," Louisa admitted. "But the flirty driver who looked prematurely bald is one of the drivers tomorrow. I'll get you on his wagon, but then it's up to you. Your husband will still be here. He's the very last pickup." She took a deep breath. "Do you want to give it a go?"

"Yes!" Phoebe clutched Louisa in a grateful hug. "Thank you from the bottom of my heart. What would I have done without you?"

Louisa grinned. "Don't thank me yet," she said. "But if you expose this driver's morphine thefts, you can hug me till there's no breath left in my body."

Phoebe laughed. Inside, she was petrified, but she knew she would have to do her best to give a first-rate performance. Her husband's life depended on it.

By that afternoon, after practicing with some crutches in their room, Phoebe was marginally more confident. She was now in George's room. She'd already changed. Louisa fixed her hair, then vanished to watch for the wagon. When it was time, Louisa would summon her. She'd go directly to the waiting wagon, hoping to escape the notice of any surgeons.

"You look fetching," George chuckled during lunch, "but it's a bit strange to see you dressed as a comrade-in-arms."

Phoebe smiled. "We've always been comrades."

He gripped her hand, his smile gone. "Stay safe."

"I will." She smiled and hoped he believed her. If he knew what she planned with those borrowed crutches, he wouldn't let her out of the room.

A sharp knock came twenty minutes later. "Time to go. He's here," Louisa hissed through the door.

Pushing down her terror, Phoebe kissed George, tucked the crutches under her armpits, and swung out into the hall.

Louisa closed the door behind her. "Your driver's already loading, checking off names as they climb aboard." She leaned near. "You're Private Caleb Marks."

Hoping she wouldn't faint, Phoebe hobbled on the crutches through the lobby to the front door.

"This is the soldier dropped here by mistake," Louisa said to the driver. "Private Caleb Marks, the last name on your list."

The driver barely glanced up as he checked off the name. Phoebe hobbled outside and waited in line at the back of the wagon. Keeping her head down and cap low, she watched the blue-clad legs in front of her.

"Here, soldier, I help you, no?" a familiar voice said behind her.

Phoebe glanced up in panic and caught the eye of Marco de Luca. His startled expression of recognition terrified her. He grabbed her elbow. "What you—"

"Shhh," Phoebe pleaded with a small shake of her head.

The medical student suddenly let go of her arm and took her crutches. Her heart sank. Her plan had failed before she even started. She wanted to weep.

But the young Italian tossed the crutches into the back of the wagon. "Step on block, soldier," he said, once again taking Phoebe's arm. "*Buona fortuna.*"

Breathless, Phoebe nodded, grateful for any "good luck"

wished on her. She clambered into the wagon and maneuvered around three soldiers to sit near the front on a bale of hay.

After the driver climbed up and flicked the reins, she glanced back. The mules started down the street while Louisa and the medical student watched.

Phoebe jounced along the potholed street, senses on full alert. They turned down an unfamiliar street. When—and how—could she expose the driver for what he was? She pushed down the fear that threatened to overwhelm her. If this deceptively cheerful ambulance driver had shot her husband in cold blood, he wouldn't hesitate to kill her.

Whatever she attempted, it had better succeed. She wouldn't get a second chance.

She kept her face down, hidden in her cap's shadow, and her shoulders hunched against the snow flurries. She feigned sleep to avoid any conversation. She feared her voice would give her away, no matter how deep she tried to make it.

They stopped next at Wiswell Barracks Post Hospital to pick up two more soldiers, one on crutches and one missing an arm. With eyes open only a slit, Phoebe watched the driver bound up onto his seat and grab the reins again. He drove the mules with one hand while he deftly slipped the other hand into his coat pocket and pulled out two brown bottles. While still staring straight ahead, he pushed the two bottles to the bottom of the haversack on the seat beside him.

Someone at that hospital had given him two bottles of drugs. Phoebe held her breath. She wanted to cry out and expose him, but a voice in her head cautioned her: *Not yet.* She had to reveal his scheme without getting herself killed in the process.

Phoebe was startled to see that the next stop was the mansion hospital where George's friend had been—James Breckinridge, the man who could have proved her husband's innocence. The man who'd disappeared without a trace.

The driver jumped down and strode up the flagstone front walk. The moment he disappeared inside, Phoebe reached over the seat to grab the driver's haversack. Keeping one eye on the front door, she lifted the leather flap and pushed her hand to the bottom.

"You!" called one of the other soldiers. "What are you doing?"

"Shh!" Phoebe begged without turning around. They couldn't get a good look at her face or all was lost.

She felt the two bottles of medicine the driver had been smuggled at the last hotel. But there were others . . . four, five, six. They might not all be morphine, but she would bet her life that they were all stolen.

When the front door opened, Phoebe closed the flap, left the haversack on the seat, and huddled in the corner of the wagon. Two soldiers on crutches came slowly down the walk, undoubtedly to make a full load. They were about to head to their final destination She had to do something *now*.

Phoebe poised to attack. An attendant helped the patients into the wagon, then turned and headed back up the walk.

"Wait!" Phoebe yelled, jumping up. "Don't go!"

The attendant whipped around at her shout, but the driver looked annoyed. "Sit down, soldier," he commanded.

Phoebe ignored him and focused on the attendant, praying he wasn't a partner in the drug scheme. "Please! Come here." She pointed at the driver. "He's stealing drugs. He shot my husband twice and left him to die."

"Husband?" The driver flinched, then jumped up onto the wagon seat and reached for his haversack. "You're delirious."

Phoebe grabbed her crutch and swung hard. The driver ducked, but she wasn't aiming for him. Her heavy wooden stick came down on the haversack. At the sound of breaking glass, she grabbed the haversack. Liquid poured out the bottom. Before she could dump out the contents for all to see, the driver grabbed her arm and twisted it. Phoebe shrieked as sharp pain ripped through her shoulder. She rammed into him and bit his arm. He tried to shake her loose, but she clung like a tigress with her prey. *How dare you steal from wounded soldiers!*

As he twisted to wrestle the haversack away from her, his sleeve gave way and ripped, revealing a muscular forearm. On the inside of his arm was a coiled rattlesnake.

Phoebe yanked back in surprise, releasing her grip on him. *A rattlesnake tattoo, just as George said.* Then something else clicked. The Italian medical student had said the driver was called Rhett, but had he misunderstood? Maybe they called him Rat, short for "rattlesnake." Most of the tattoos she'd seen on soldiers were patriotic symbols or names of wives and sweethearts. But a rattlesnake was fitting for a man who made a profit out of other people's misery.

In the split second that Phoebe hesitated, the driver swung at her, knocking off her cap. Her long hair tumbled down, to the shocked cries of the other soldiers.

"Help me!" Phoebe cried.

The attendant watched but didn't move. Phoebe knew she looked like a crazy woman who'd disguised herself and attacked the driver for some unimaginable reason.

Just then, a nurse came running down the walkway. "Help that woman!" she ordered.

The ambulance driver glanced toward the new voice, and Phoebe grabbed again at the haversack and upended it. Liquid dripped and pills spilled out onto the seat and bounced over the side of the wagon.

The nurse—the one Phoebe had accosted last night—gave the attendant a shove. "Help her. Stop him!"

She'd galvanized him into action. He and a soldier overpowered the driver, pinning his arms behind him. "What's he done?" the attendant asked.

The nurse met Phoebe's eye, and understanding passed between them. "This driver," the nurse said, "and one of our doctors are stealing morphine our patients need and selling it for their own profit. I've been forced to get painkillers for my own patients from my father, a surgeon in another hospital."

"That's true," Phoebe said. "My husband saw this driver take morphine at Fredericksburg. The driver shot my husband to keep him quiet, then reported him as a deserter. When I tried to clear my husband's name, I believe he stole my evidence." She appealed to the attendant. "Please bring this man back to the Union Hotel Hospital for my husband to identify."

After the driver was tied up and unceremoniously thrown into the back of the wagon, his haversack was searched and the drugs confiscated. Surrounded by five angry soldiers, many with long wooden crutches, the "rat" was subdued.

Phoebe sat on the seat beside the attendant, who now drove the ambulance wagon. *Hurry, hurry!* she wanted to shout. She had to get back before George was hauled off to prison. She'd finally proved the driver was stealing morphine.

Then a horrible thought occurred to her.

When it came to the shooting—how and where it had occurred—it was still the ambulance driver's word against her husband's. She'd proved the driver was a thief, but she hadn't proved that George wasn't a deserter. Not at all.

20

Washington, D.C.
January 1863

When Phoebe stepped through the front door of the hospital, still wearing a Yankee uniform and with her long hair tumbling down her back, mouths dropped open. Those in the lobby stopped and stared, first at her appearance, and then at the tied-up driver being manhandled inside by the attendant.

Phoebe strode into the ballroom ward, looking for Louisa. Before she found her, a round of applause broke out. Puzzled, Phoebe glanced around the ward, then realized what a sight she presented; they must think her an exceptionally patriotic wife. Blushing, she gathered her long hair and twisted it, but she'd lost the pins that had held it up. She finally gave up and let it cascade around her shoulders.

Louisa hurried over and followed Phoebe into the lobby. After spotting the driver who waited sullenly near the staircase, she hugged Phoebe so hard that she lifted her off her feet. "You did it!"

"Thanks to your disguise." Phoebe grinned. "I must go tell George."

"Wait," Louisa said. "Let me get him. Then you can tell everyone what happened—and how you proved that your husband is no liar. He deserves to hear the good news in front of the men who were told he's a deserter."

Phoebe considered her words. Maybe Louisa was right.

Louisa grabbed a wheelchair in the hallway. Five minutes later she returned, pushing George. Her husband spotted the ambulance driver immediately. The driver's lip curled back in a sneer. George nodded. "Yes. That's him."

The driver snarled, "Just your word against mine."

Phoebe bent to hug her husband. Then she followed Louisa into the ballroom ward. She told her story as the wounded soldiers listened in total silence. She explained how her husband had been shot because of what he saw, how she'd hunted for James Breckinridge to back up George's story and how James had disappeared, how George had been intentionally infected with typhus, and how Dr. Bertram's daughter had said drugs were being stolen from her hospital too.

As her story unfolded, Phoebe noticed two expressions on the soldiers' faces. One was a softening toward her husband—or maybe it was shame that they'd believed George was a traitor. The other was a hardening as her tale of conspiracy unfolded, anger at how painkillers they desperately needed had been stolen and sold to the highest bidder.

Phoebe scowled at the bound driver. "If you know what's good for you, you will tell the authorities who you were working with in this hospital."

She turned to the soldiers gathered in the lobby. "My husband has suffered needlessly because of that driver, first from two bullet wounds, and then by being labeled a coward and deserter."

Someone cleared his throat behind her. Young Marco de Luca stepped forward from where he'd been listening in the doorway. "I also say how sorry all doctors feel for poor treatment to Mr. Ashford. We are *nel suo debito*, in his debt."

The soldiers remained silent, but Phoebe was satisfied with the sympathy and respect on their faces. Surely George wouldn't go to prison now; he would be brought to the main ward with more heat, better food, and the company of his comrades. When he was ready, he would go to a convalescent home—or maybe even to their home. Phoebe wanted to break out in a dance. Oh, how bright the new year felt now! She turned to watch the disgraced trafficker being led away by the military police.

Phoebe pushed her husband back to his cubbyhole room to talk privately and pack his few possessions for his move to one of the wards. Though she was exhausted enough to drop in her tracks, she was also exhilarated. They talked for an hour. Dr. Bertram checked his wounds and humbly apologized for the ill treatment he had received.

Early that evening, as Phoebe gathered up her husband's belongings to help move him to the ward, she let her heart dwell on home. Both Christmas and New Year's had come and gone, but it didn't matter. They'd celebrate late this year. "We'll go home as soon as you can travel," she said. "You can heal there."

"I wish that were possible, Phoebe." His face clouded over then. "But you must be realistic. The army won't drop the desertion charge, even though we found the drug ring. Regrettably, that scum driver is right. He can still claim he found me north of here, running away."

Phoebe's throat constricted until she couldn't breathe. *After all we've been through!* It was so unfair.

George gripped both her hands in his. "We must face it. It's still the driver's word against mine."

"Not anymore," said a deep voice from the doorway. "Now it's *our* word against his."

"James!" George cried, his face alight. "Where did you come from?" He glanced at Phoebe.

"I had nothing to do with this," Phoebe said. "If this is James Breckinridge, I've no idea how he got here." She stood up and held out her hand to her husband's friend. "But you're the most welcome sight we can imagine." He limped into the tiny room, and Phoebe pulled up her chair for him.

Looking up, Phoebe spotted the Italian medical student lurking out in the hallway and stepped out to speak to him. "Did you bring James Breckinridge here?"

He shrugged. "Nurse Alcott, she tells me this man's story *importante*, no? If he is alive."

"Very important. But how did you find him?"

"I go to hospital of Nurse Bertram. She tells me bad surgeon sends James Breckinridge away after he says driver shoots his friend in back. The surgeon sends him to a . . ." He waved a hand as he searched for words. "A *casa di convalescenza*, er, convalescent home outside city. I hire cab for to pick him up."

"Yes!" Phoebe wanted to dance a jig down the hallway and back. "You have no idea how much this means to my husband and to me." She glanced over her shoulder at George and James, who were deep in conversation. "James will vouch for George and clear his name. My husband won't go to prison. But that scummy driver and all of his conspirators will!"

Nearly a week later, Phoebe packed up so she and George could catch the afternoon train home to Vermont. They'd missed the holidays with the children, but no one would mind celebrating late. They'd been given the best Christmas gift ever: George's freedom. The accusation of desertion had been dropped with James's testimony, and George had been given a month's leave to recuperate at home.

Doubly sweet, Nurse Alcott had told Phoebe that the driver

had revealed that Dr. Kauffmann, the surly physician from the Union Hotel Hospital, had been his contact for morphine stolen from there. It had been Dr. Kauffmann who had sneaked into Phoebe's room and stolen her evidence.

Phoebe packed food for the journey and cleaned the room she'd shared with Louisa while George said goodbye to his new friends in the ward. The last thing she folded to pack was the quilt Jane had sewn and sent to George. She studied the center silk square made from scraps of a Green Mountain Boys blue-and-green flag.

She considered the Italian medical student, far from home and family, who had done so much for her and her husband. She wished she could do more than say thank you.

Then she smiled at the idea that crossed her mind. Jane would applaud her plan after she heard about the part he'd played in George's rescue. Phoebe found Marco outside a surgery room. "We're leaving now," she said.

"To go home?" His black eyes danced with joy for her.

"Yes." She held out the quilt. "It is a small thing, but I want you to have this."

He tilted his head quizzically.

"To thank you for your help."

Marco made a slight bow. "Very welcome. Maybe you come to my village someday?"

Phoebe smiled, but she knew it was extremely unlikely that she and George would ever travel to Marco's village on the Italian coast. However, the quilt—and their gratitude and prayers—could go with him.

Cabot Falls, Vermont
Present Day

Sofia's dining-room table was covered with color photos and brochures. Instead of painting that evening, the Pinot Painters had met in the afternoon to sort through the pictures taken at the St. Albans reenactment a few days before. Sofia had loved photographing the outdoor church service and the women's fancy dresses on the second day of the reenactment. Julie had taken photos of the battles and cavalry charges. Marla had covered both the Union and Confederate camps. Sofia's only regret was she hadn't taken photos of her ladies' tea.

One of her favorite pictures, though, was a photo of the Lincoln impersonator with Luke. Sofia had taken to heart the actor's gentle warning about "a house divided." She'd talked it out with Jim when they'd arrived home, forgiven him—and herself—and let it go.

"Should we all paint the same scenes," Marla asked, "or should we each paint our own specific events?"

They were following through on their idea to paint reenactment scenes for the tourists: some small framed pictures, some scenes on crocks or mugs, and some on rough barn wood.

"Let's divide the photos up while we eat," Julie said. "I missed my lunch—work was just crazy—and I could practically inhale those little desserts you made."

"These were the most popular ones at the tea," Sofia said, passing out dessert plates. "I made a few more from the leftover ingredients. Eat what you want before the kids get home from school."

While she ate a raspberry tart, Sofia unfolded a brochure she'd picked up at the quilt display in the brick hall. Inside was a photo of the famous quilt made by the Vermont woman, Jane Stickle, whom Amanda had impersonated so well. She gasped as she read. "The back of the quilt is stitched with *Signed in wartime, 1863.*" She held it up to show her friends.

Marla swallowed a bite. "What is it? Your voice sounds funny."

"And you've gone pale," Julie added.

"That's what the bottom edge of *my* quilt square says. You know, the one I'm researching now."

"*Signed in wartime, 1863?*" Julie asked.

"Well, mine says 1862, but it's made of blue and green silk too. Jane Stickle's blue-and-green squares were made from the tattered flags of the Green Mountain Boys in Vermont. Do you think this famous quilter made *my* square?"

Marla frowned. "Don't you suppose lots of Vermont war widows did that with their loved ones' flags?"

Julie reached for another cream-filled biscuit. "If this famous Jane Stickle from Vermont made your square, how did it end up in your Italian grandmother's quilt?"

"I have no idea, and I'm probably wrong," Sofia said, "but it's quite a coincidence."

"Can't you computer whizzes research it or something?" Julie licked creamy filling from her manicured nails.

"Yes, I did some this week," Marla said, "but the information in the diary is very sketchy on this square. It did give a city in Italy—"

"Positano," Sofia interjected.

"—and the name of a hotel, but my research hasn't revealed much." She reached for her purse and pulled out some folded papers. "I printed out everything I found. I'm not sure it will help."

"Thank you." Sofia glanced at the clock. School would be out soon, so she'd read Marla's research after the kids were tucked into bed that night. She'd have no chance to commandeer the laptop until then anyway.

That night, the October air turned nippy, and Sofia curled up under an afghan in the living room after the kids' bedtime. Jim was grading papers at the dining-room table, so she had the computer to herself. She scanned the notes in her spiral notebook, her translated words and phrases from Nonna's leather-covered journal, and began her search.

The Italian village named Positano was located by the sea. The first name in the diary—Febe—could be an ancestor. Sofia could only find a Union Hotel overseas in the Swiss city of Bellinzona, located at the foot of the Alps. She found no city of Fredericksburg whatsoever, except in the United States. She was no longer sure that her quilt square had anything to do with the Green Mountain Boys. And the only Marco de Luca biographies she found were modern, half a dozen of them on Facebook alone.

Sofia sighed.

"That was a big sigh," Jim called from the dining room. "Anything the matter?"

"Oh, just that Julie was right. An Italian named Febe who might or might not be from the village of Positano probably has no bearing on the American Civil War."

"Whatever made you think he did?"

"My square closely resembles the center square of a quilt I saw in a brochure by the famous lady Amanda was impersonating. It has similar writing on it."

"Mmm-hmm."

Sofia smiled. He'd already gone back to grading papers.

She grabbed her notebook and pencil again. No matter how wonderful the Internet was, she still needed to write things down and draw arrows to make connections. She sensed at some gut level that the blue-and-green square from her ancestor was connected to the American Civil War. But how?

Sofia would bet her last pastry that Jane Stickle had created her silk quilt square in blue and green. If Jane were her ancestor, she would be proud to claim her. She'd stitched her way through the Civil War, waiting for her absent husband to come home alive. Sofia had struggled not knowing where Matthew was for a few hours; how had women endured when loved ones were missing for *months*?

Before she could claim Jane as an ancestor, though, she'd have to find solid links between her, Febe, and Positano, Italy. So far, there was nothing.

Well, she had all night.

For the next forty minutes, Sofia read articles about Jane Stickle, searching for a reference to a trip to Italy. There wasn't one. From what Sofia read, Jane Stickle hadn't even left Vermont, much less the country.

She did find one interesting tidbit, whether it fit into her puzzle or not. When researching the Union Hotel, one link led her to a Union Hotel in Washington, D.C. The article mentioned that it had been converted to a hospital during the Civil War and became somewhat renowned because of the author Louisa May Alcott. Sofia's breath quickened when she read the next line. Alcott had been a nurse at the hotel during the war, caring for overflow wounded from the battle at Fredericksburg, Virginia, in 1862.

Fredericksburg. 1862. Sofia continued to read.

Alcott had written a book about her experiences at the Union Hotel Hospital called *Hospital Sketches*. It had been published before *Little Women,* the book that made her famous. Did that have any bearing on her quilt square? There was no mention of Louisa May Alcott having been a quilter.

When Jim finished his grading ten minutes later, she was still reading. "You going to do that all night?" he wanted to know.

"Only a bit longer."

"I'll lock up," Jim said, kissing the top of her head as she bent over the laptop.

Sofia nodded and decided to come at her research from a different angle, starting with the Italian names of Positano and Febe. She wished she could read the websites that Marla could access as head librarian.

"Oh, good grief!" she moaned.

"Now what?" Jim called from the front hall.

"Nothing. Just a memory lapse." She ran to the kitchen and searched high and low. What had she done with the pages Marla had given her? She finally found them stashed in a drawer with the kids' school calendars. She must have shoved them in there when cleaning up during the hubbub after school.

Back in the living room, Sofia pored over the typed pages. Marla had found Marco de Luca through two primary ancestry sites. He'd been a doctor in Positano. His birth and death dates proved that he had been alive during the time Jane Stickle was quilting and waiting for her husband's return from the war.

She flipped to the second page, and then the third. Marco de Luca had gone to medical school in Philadelphia, enrolling before the Civil War broke out. *He was in America.*

She read feverishly then, forcing herself to read every single word when her eyes wanted to skip ahead by leaps and bounds. *Patience, patience.*

At last she found what she was searching for. *His medical training was interrupted by the war,* Marla had written. *Rather than returning to Italy, de Luca accompanied his instructor, a Dr. Bertram, and received on-the-job training by assisting the good doctor first on the battlefields, then in a two-year stint at the Union Hotel Hospital in Washington, D.C. Dr. de Luca obtained his license and returned home in 1865 to marry his childhood sweetheart, who had waited out the American Civil War back in Positano. She was his nurse and wife for forty-three years.*

Sofia tried to keep calm, but she sensed she was very close to the answer. This put the Italian from Nonna's diary in America during the war in 1862. Her quilt square signed that year was in the identical colors and materials used in Jane Stickle's famous quilt. But had Jane Stickle and Marco de Luca ever met so he could have ended up with the quilt square? So far, her research—and Marla's—said no.

Frustrated and feeling a bit defeated, Sofia went to reheat a cup of chamomile tea in the microwave. A minute later, back at the Jane Stickle biography sites, she went through the longest profile with a fine-toothed comb. Then, near the end, she found something that made her heart race: *Although Jane and her husband had no children of their own,* the article read, *for a brief time she had the sole care of two children while her best friend, Phoebe Ashford, went to nurse her wounded husband at the Union Hotel Hospital in Washington, D.C. Jane donated many quilts to the "brave boys in blue," and Mrs. Ashford took one for her husband, but it is unknown what became of it.*

Something clicked, and Sofia went back through her notes to her original translation of Nonna's diary. *Yes.* There had been a lone Italian first name, Febe. Holding her breath, she searched online for translations of Italian names. And there it was. *Febe* was the Italian name for Phoebe.

Here she had the missing link. Her quilt square *had* been made by the famous Jane Stickle. It must have been part of the quilt given to Phoebe Ashford for her wounded husband. Somehow the young medical student, Marco de Luca, who had been at the same hospital at the same time as the Ashfords, ended up with it. A gift of gratitude for saving Phoebe's husband's life, perhaps? He probably would have brought it home to Italy along with his American medical degree.

Sofia sat back on the couch and soaked in her victory.

Marco de Luca and his wife must be her ancestors on Nonna's side, but the quilt square had been pieced by a world-famous quilter who'd lived just over a hundred miles from Cabot Falls.

Sofia nodded and closed the laptop. All of them—Jane Stickle, Phoebe Ashford, Marco de Luca, and his wife—had survived the pain and hardship of separation during war. On a small scale, Sofia could understand that, having been separated from Matthew during that long, hard day. They had endured, and each was a hero in her eyes. "Heroism is endurance for one moment more." The quote from historian George F. Kennan sprang unbidden to her mind.

Sofia stood and stretched, folded the afghan, then switched off the table lamp. She hoped that she, too, would run her own life's race with such strength. She'd been given courageous footsteps to follow.

Learn more about Annie's fiction books at

AnniesFiction.com

- Access your e-books
- Discover exciting new series
- Read sample chapters
- Watch video book trailers
- Share your feedback

We've designed the Annie's Fiction website especially for you!

Plus, manage your account online!

- Check your account status
- Make payments online
- Update your address

Visit us at AnniesFiction.com